"Let's be straight with each other, Heather," Josh said. **"There are some interesting sparks between us, aren't there?"**

She was too honest to try and deny his claim, but his unexpected display of arrogance irked her. "Sparks don't have to start major conflagrations," she said, then swallowed hard as she saw dangerous golden flames in Josh's eyes and felt the fires of response deep inside herself.

Josh cradled her face between his hands and bent to brush his lips over hers. "But some sparks do," he murmured, then toyed with her mouth, deliberately and expertly teasing her until he felt her breathing become ragged, her arms twining around his neck. He told himself Heather needed to learn to be less trusting of men like Josh Campbell. She had to be taught how vulnerable she was.

Heather tried to summon resistance to Josh's kiss, but her will was paralyzed, overruled by a sudden need she'd never dreamed could grip her. She wanted only to feel Josh, to taste him, breathe in his tantalizing scent, mold her body to his. It was the most exciting yet most terrifying moment she'd ever experienced.

At the same instant Josh realized the lesson he'd meant to give had backfired. Wrapping his arms around Heather's body, he felt suddenly dizzy. "Heather," he whispered, releasing her lips for a moment to gaze at her in utter shock. "What are you doing to me?" Then both were lost to pure sensation. . . .

WHAT ARE *LOVESWEPT* ROMANCES?

They are stories of true romance and touching emotion. We believe those two very important ingredients are constants in our highly sensual and very believable stories in the *LOVESWEPT* line. Our goal is to give you, the reader, stories of consistently high quality that may sometimes make you laugh, sometimes make you cry, but are always fresh and creative and contain many delightful surprises within their pages.

Most romance fans read an enormous number of books. Those they truly love, they keep. Others may be traded with friends and soon forgotten. We hope that each *LOVESWEPT* romance will be a treasure—a "keeper." We will always try to publish

LOVE STORIES YOU'LL NEVER FORGET
BY AUTHORS YOU'LL ALWAYS REMEMBER

The Editors

LOVESWEPT® · 385

Gail Douglas
The Dreamweavers:
Bewitching Lady

BANTAM BOOKS
NEW YORK · TORONTO · LONDON · SYDNEY · AUCKLAND

THE DREAMWEAVERS: BEWITCHING LADY

A Bantam Book / March 1990

If you would be interested in receiving protective vinyl
covers for your Loveswept books, please write to this address
for information:

Loveswept
Bantam Books
P.O. Box 985
Hicksville, NY 11802

ISBN 0-553-44000-4

Published simultaneously in the United States and Canada

PRINTED IN THE UNITED STATES OF AMERICA

OPM   0 9 8 7 6 5 4 3 2 1

To James,
my Knight of the Scottish Isle

One

"You really are—ouch!—such a twit," Heather Sinclair chided herself as she picked her way down the thistle-strewn embankment toward the gurgling brook she'd spotted from the road.

But all the scratches on her bare legs and the burdocks caught on her skirt seemed worthwhile once she was sitting on the low riverbank, soothing her feet in the cool stream.

Actually, the stream wasn't just cool, Heather thought as she shivered a little; it was melted snow from far up in the Highlands, and it was like ice. Nevertheless, it was a healing balm to her blistered, cut, burning feet.

Little by little, Heather shifted forward to brave the chilly waters up to her calves, the aches and soreness temporarily relieved by the numbness that soon set in. "Twit," she said again, plucking at the burdocks that had attached themselves to the low hemline of her full denim skirt. "Next time you decide to go for a long walk, try wearing jeans and a pair of sneakers," she muttered. "And socks. Thick cotton socks. You should know better than to go wandering off the beaten track with nothing on your feet but skimpy sandals."

In the distance, a cuckoo put in its two cents worth, repeating its insulting call several times, as if to be sure Heather got the point.

Laughing, Heather leaned back on her palms, closed her eyes, and raised her face to the sliver of warm May sun still unobscured by the afternoon's gathering clouds.

For several moments she was too relaxed to worry about the rest of the trek ahead. Lulled into a semi-trance by the whisper of dancing blades of grass and the childlike giggle of a rivulet sneaking past a cluster of submerged rocks, Heather became aware only gradually of a sprinkle of soft rain, and then, a moment later, of a low rumble from up on the road.

As the sound grew louder, Heather's eyes snapped open. A car was coming. Perhaps even a bus.

Suddenly the shower began in earnest, and Heather decided she'd better get up to the road and try to catch a ride from whoever was approaching.

Jumping to her feet, grateful that they were still numb to pain, Heather grabbed her sandals, pulled her paisley shawl over her head, and scrambled up the rough ground of the slope, reaching the top just in time to wave her arms wildly at the blue Austin that was almost upon her.

Hitchhiking wasn't something she did often, but at the moment it seemed like a fine idea.

The squeal of brakes made Heather grin with a twinge of both amusement and guilt as she realized that her sudden leap onto the side of the road had given the driver a dreadful start.

He was out of the car in the next second, looming over her and glowering like an enraged titan.

"Where in blazes did you come from?" he demanded in a deep voice that seemed to roll up from his broad chest like thunder over Loch Lomond.

Slowly looking up at the man, her eyes wide, Heather couldn't say a word. She was gripped by a strange rush of inexplicable anxiety that seemed rooted in an elusive memory. All she could do was gape at him in rapt admiration.

Josh Campbell pushed splayed fingers through his straw-blond hair, trying to collect his wits. The girl had materialized from nowhere, as if she'd stepped out of some mythical village, some Brigadoon that rose up out of the mist only once every hundred years.

She was the epitome of a Scottish country lass from an era lost in time, the kind of girl whose name would be Fiona or Morag. She was tall and slender, her skin almost translucently pale, her red-gold hair peeking out from under her shawl to curl damply around her heart-shaped face, her legs and feet bare, her eyes a dark evergreen that seemed to see mysteries beyond Josh's vision.

For a brief, unnerving moment, he wondered if he'd slipped back into the fevered delirium that had held his mind captive just months before.

Becoming self-conscious under the girl's scrutiny, feeling as though she could see his scars, Josh barked out his question again. "Where did you come from?"

Heather swallowed hard and blinked, continuing to stare up at him even as she pointed over her shoulder with her thumb in the general direction of the stream. "Down there," she murmured.

Josh's throat was constricted, and he didn't know why. He blamed his strange tension on the fright the girl had given him. "Don't you know better than to jump in front of a car?" he asked. "I could have run over you!"

His words brought Heather out of her little trance, and she smiled quizzically. "I didn't jump in front of your car. I waved from right here on the side of the road, so there was no danger at all. I do thank you for stoppin', though." Unconsciously, she'd spoken with the hint of a Scottish lilt that crept into her speech when she was slightly flustered.

"Are you alone?" Josh asked, checking the terrain beyond her as the thought of modern-day highwaymen crossed his mind; it wouldn't be the first time an innocent-looking female had been used as a lure for potential victims.

The man was an American, Heather thought with a mixture of pleasure and regret. It was always a happy surprise to encounter a compatriot, but the very fact that her rescuer was from the States meant that he most likely was only a visitor to Scotland—which, she hastily reminded herself, was just as well. She couldn't imagine what had gotten into her to be so taken with a man like this one, a big, brawny Yank who looked as if he could wield a claymore like any seventeenth-century clansman—though the jeans hugging his taut thighs and lean hips were decidedly modern and every bit as appealing as a kilt.

Heather's gaze moved over him, taking in the pale yellow Shetland sweater that casually enhanced his wide shoulders and massive chest. He'd pushed up the sleeves almost to the elbows, revealing muscular forearms tanned to a warm golden hue and matted with sun-bleached hair, a complicated-looking watch at his wrist.

He had a wonderfully craggy face, Heather mused as she continued her once-over, taking in the man's prominent cheekbones, wide-set eyes, high forehead, and a jaw worthy of the most obdurate of Scots. She thought his face might have been a touch too perfect once, perhaps before someone or something had rearranged it just enough to make it more interesting.

His eyes captivated her most of all. If they weren't quite windows to his soul, their hazel depths did hint at secret passageways, their colors changing like the mysterious stone of a mood ring. At this particular moment they were a dark bronze that snapped with anger and a dollop of suspicion.

For a delicious instant, Heather was a Saxon maiden of another millenium, faced with a virile Norse raider. Her heartbeat took a few playful skips; she was tempted to offer herself as a hostage to save the rest of her village.

But the twentieth century forced its way back into her consciousness and she remembered that this man's brand of raw masculinity wasn't for her. He didn't remotely resemble the man of her dreams. He couldn't possibly be The One. She mustn't start weaving him into the costume dramas of her imagination.

"Don't you answer questions?" Josh asked impatiently, wishing the girl would quit looking at him with such unsettling intensity. She seemed young—perhaps in her late teens—but she certainly wasn't afflicted with adolescent shyness.

Though Heather didn't blame the man for being cranky, considering the turn she'd given him, she couldn't resist a bit of teasing. Besides, a touch of cheekiness always helped her cover emotions she wanted kept private. "Aye, I'm alone," she told him, deliberately reverting to her Scottish accent and exaggerating it for good measure. "Except, of course, for a wee cuckoo back there who's been mockin' me for the past few minutes—which I truly didn't mind a bit, because as you probably know, it's lucky to be out walkin' when you hear your first cuckoo of a new spring. Then, too, there were some water sprites who invited me to cool the soreness of my feet in the burn that flows under that bridge just ahead. And, of course, we mustn't forget the fairy folk."

Josh frowned. "Fairy folk?" he echoed, looking askance at the smiling girl.

"Och, aye," Heather said. "It's May, don't you know. After bein' cooped up all the long winter months, the little creatures have been let out just today by the King of the Fairies, to celebrate the comin' of spring. They're singin' and dancin' and fiddlin' and generally havin' themselves a grand old ceilidh."

Josh suppressed an unbidden smile. He wasn't sure whether the young lady believed her own nonsense or was putting him on. He suspected the latter. There was too much merriment in her face for him to believe she was sincere. Her green eyes glinted with too much humor. Her mouth was twitching too dangerously. Even her wayward curls looked mischievous. He couldn't resist playing along with her nonsense. "So you and your water sprites and fairy folk were having yourselves a ball, were you? Not to mention the lucky cuckoo."

"Aye," Heather answered with a grin. "But now I have to be on my way, and I need a wee bit of transportation, if you'd be so kind."

Josh didn't hesitate. He couldn't very well leave the minx out in the rain. Going around to the passenger side, he opened the car door and motioned with an inclination of his head. "Get in," he said with sudden gruffness as it hit him how dangerously naive it was of the girl to hitch a ride with a total stranger.

"Thanks ever so much," Heather said, adding a little curtsy before she hurried as best she could around the car, hoping her limp wasn't too noticeable. She couldn't seem to help it now that the feeling had returned to her feet.

"Where are you going?" Josh asked when they were on their way.

"Dunfermline," Heather answered as she took off her shawl and folded it. "At least that's where I was headed or hoped I was headed, but any town would do, or even a main road where I could catch a bus."

"I'll take you to Dunfermline. It's not far." Turning to glance at the girl, Josh scowled, determined to convey his disapproval. "Not far to drive, anyway. But to walk? Barefoot?"

Heather grinned at him, deciding to admit her folly. "I didn't start out barefoot." She held up her sandals. "I was in Alva Glen; I'd taken a bus there, you see. My goodness, it was one bus after the other, to all the places I wanted to visit today to test out a walking tour my friend Maharg told me my clients would enjoy. But wouldn't you know, I missed the bus I planned to go back home on, so I started out on foot, thinkin' another would be along. It seems I was mistaken, or perhaps took a wrong turn and ended up on this road where there appear to be no buses at all, and precious few cars, I must say. I'm truly grateful that you came along just when you did, sir. Strictly speakin', though, I'm not on my way to Dunfermline."

Josh barely kept from laughing aloud at the barrage of words that tumbled from the girl's soft, pretty mouth, and he found his curiosity piqued by practically every statement she tossed off. But first things first, he decided. "Exactly where is it you do want to go?" he asked, adding with a grin, "Strictly speakin'."

"Well, in the general direction of Edinburgh," Heather answered, then hastily said, "but I'd never ask you to—"

"I'm on my way to Edinburgh," Josh interrupted. "I'll drive you home."

"I couldn't let you," Heather said. "The thing is, I don't live right in Edinburgh."

Josh took a deep breath, then spoke in measured syllables. "Would you like to tell me precisely where you *do* want to go?"

Heather realized she'd lapsed into her irritating habit of giving convoluted answers to simple questions. "Well, as I said, I couldn't let you drive me home, for I live in a village on this bank of the Firth of Forth, but a wee bit on the other side of the Forth bridge, which I'm sure you'd be wantin' to take into the city."

"Just direct me when we get close to the bridge," Josh stated firmly. "I'll drive you to your door." He paused to glare at her. "And perhaps I'll go in with you to suggest to your parents that you should be grounded until you learn not to get yourself into a situation where you have to accept a ride from a strange man."

To Josh's puzzled dismay, the girl tipped back her head and laughed with infectious delight. The sound did something strange to his insides. "What's so funny?" he muttered. "Are Scottish parents as permissive as most of the ones I know back in the States? Do they let their daughters do whatever they like, go wherever they wish, even if it isn't safe?"

"Just what age do you take me for?" she asked, thoroughly amused.

Josh's glance slid over her. He would put her somewhere between sixteen and eighteen, though she would have to be a particularly mature sixteen, he had to concede as he belatedly took in her incredibly long, shapely legs and the generous breasts pressing against her red shell top, the tips pouting visibly under the thin cotton.

Quickly looking away, Josh arrested the direction of his thoughts. What was wrong with him? He wasn't in the habit of lusting after teenagers. Why, this creature actually had a dusting of freckles over her pert nose! And no female who'd left her adolescence behind could look so innocently sensual.

"I'd say you're about fifteen," he answered at last, deliberately subtracting a year from his lowest estimate, certain that young girls hated a low guess as much as they would someday deplore a high one.

"Fifteen!" she repeated, then laughed again. "Och, indeed! You're not only bonny, you're just as charmin' a lad as ever I've had the pleasure of meetin'."

For the second time, Josh felt his insides doing a couple of odd contractions. That laugh was getting to him. It was so husky. Throaty. Filled with irrepressible humor. It crossed his mind that some of the bad days he'd been through during the past months might have seemed less bleak if he'd been exposed to such a contagious sound.

But this foolish girl shouldn't go around laughing at strange men, calling them *bonny* and *charmin'*, Josh thought. And the way she'd stared at him a while ago, when he'd first gotten out of the car—somebody had to tell her she was courting trouble. "You're a bold little thing," he said.

"Bold, am I?" she said, her voice quivering with delight. "And will you say so to Mum and Dad?"

Josh kept his eyes on the lonely road as if it were the Grand Prix route at the climax of a hard-fought race. "Maybe I should," he answered tightly. "Maybe someone ought to have a word with your folks. What's your name, anyway?"

"Heather Sinclair," she said pleasantly.

Heather, Josh thought with a reluctant smile. The name was even more right for the girl than Fiona or Morag. "Tell me, Heather, do you often take rides with strangers?"

"Never," Heather answered, resting her elbow on the back of the seat, turning her body slightly sideways so she could study the sturdy Scots look of this American who was so oddly appealing, even if he was the exact opposite of the kind of man who filled her particular romantic requirements.

Acutely aware of the girl's frank gaze, Josh concentrated on scolding her. "Never? You claim you never take rides with strangers? What do you call getting into my car? And what kind of man is most likely to stop and pick up a pretty young girl, anyway? Some character who'll dish out more than you can handle, that's what kind."

"Do you really think I'm pretty?" Heather asked, a smile playing at the corners of her mouth.

Josh turned to look at her, caught completely off guard. The question of whether or not this girl was pretty hadn't crossed his mind on a conscious level. It seemed irrelevant. He couldn't see past the glow of her vibrant personality to think about mere prettiness. She was luminous. She was captivating. She was—Josh wasn't sure what she was. But the word *pretty* definitely fell short of an adequate description. Nevertheless, he nodded and said gravely, "Of course you're pretty. All young girls are, in their own way."

"How sweet," Heather murmured, amused by his diplomacy.

"You still haven't answered me," Josh shot back. "If you don't make a habit of thumbing rides with strangers, how do you explain hitching one with me?"

"That's easy," Heather answered. "You're no stranger. I knew right away you were trustworthy."

"You didn't know any such thing, young lady."

"Fate would never have sent you for me if you were a Black Knight instead of a Lancelot," Heather said, then frowned. "No, it's wrong of me to put it that way. It sounds too grand, as if Fate had nothing better to do than rescue me from one of my silly scrapes. What's more likely is that I wouldn't have heard your car comin' along the road if you were bent on some evil deed." She tried not to grin. "The fairies would have made a wild din, fiddlin' their wee hearts out so you'd have sped right on past without me bein' any the wiser, and I'd still be down at the burn soakin' my feet in its cool runnin' water."

Josh couldn't resist a glance at the girl. He wasn't at all surprised to see pure naughtiness glimmering in her big green eyes. "I have a feeling you're an incorrigible tease, Heather Sinclair."

Heather simply smiled. "Wouldna you say it's time you introduced yourself, sir?" she asked, still playing her make-believe role as a Scots lassie, her accent from neither Edinburgh nor Glasgow, neither Highland or Lowland. She wasn't trying to be authentic; she was simply having fun. "What would you be callin' yourself?"

"Ten kinds of a fool for taking on a responsibility like you," Josh said, not quite able to sound as disgruntled as he wanted to. For some reason, the depression he'd been battling for so long seemed to have lifted of its own accord.

"A responsibility, am I?" Heather said, chuckling, thinking that if he were even a tiny bit more like her dream hero, she wouldn't mind having this great strapping fellow take her under his wing. It would be a warm, lovely place to be. "Only if you had saved my life would I be your responsibility, and I'm sorry to tell you that here in Scotland the simple act of givin' a neighbor a ride doesn't qualify for lifesavin'. Nevertheless, it's good of you, Mr. Whoever-You-Are."

"My name's Josh," he said, his lips twitching with a grin he just couldn't suppress. The girl had a winning way about her, for all her flightiness. "Josh Campbell."

Heather gasped, pretending to be shocked out of her wits, cupping her palms over her cheeks in dismay. "Campbell! Och, what a calamity! A Campbell! It seems the fairies weren't payin' attention after all! You're tellin' me I've let myself be captured by a Campbell!"

"Let me guess," Josh drawled resignedly. He'd grown rather weary of the ribbing he'd taken about his name since he'd come to Scotland. "There's a MacDonald branch on your family tree, right? I suppose one of my ancestors massacred one of yours at Glencoe a couple of centuries or so ago."

"Worse," Heather said in a low, confidential tone. "I'm a MacGregor on my mother's side, sworn enemies of you Campbells, and for good reason, too, though my friend Maharg says the ancient feudin' is a lot of foolishness, and he should know, he bein' about as foolish as they come. But it's a wonder the ghosts of my forebears haven't thrown a bolt of lightnin' at me already, just for climbin' into your car. It's their own fault, though, for not warnin' me about you, Mr. Campbell."

"I understand that the MacDonalds and Mac-Gregors of old are guilty of their own share of massacres," Josh said, defending his name more for the stimulation of the banter than because he took Heather's comments seriously.

"It wasn't the massacre that bothered everyone so much," Heather said with a self-righteous sniff and a lift of her chin. "It was the abuse of hospitality. Those traitorous Campbells—sorry to say it to you, but that's the truth of it—were housed and fed by the good-hearted generosity of old Ian MacDonald of Glencoe, and what did those scoundrels do but turn upon the great MacIan in the dead of night! There's no excuse for breakin' the unspoken bond between a host and a guest."

"I couldn't agree more," Josh said with a lazy grin. "So how is it that you're a guest in my car, yet you're heaping insults on me?"

"You're right!" Heather said, her eyes wide with feigned horror. "I'm as bad as a Campbell—if you'll pardon my sayin' so. And Maharg says the carnage at Glencoe might well have been much worse, had it been the Camerons let loose on the Mac— Stop the car!"

Josh hit the brake, then cursed as the car swerved to a screeching halt on the wet road. "What's with you?" he demanded, turning to glare at Heather. "Are you nuts? Or do you just like testing my reflexes? It'll be a wonder if I don't end this day with whiplash, for Pete's—" Suddenly he stopped talking, dazzled into silence by Heather's beguiling smile.

"Look," she said, pointing toward the hill behind him, beyond his side of the road.

Josh's glance scanned the field until he saw the tawny, sleek form of a young deer loping up the slope. Josh swallowed hard. "It crossed in front of the car," he said in a low voice. "I might have hit that animal. I should've had my eyes on the road, dammit."

Realizing how shaken he was by the near miss, Heather regretted the nonsense that had diverted his attention from his driving. "Oh, it wasn't as close a call as it seemed," she said gently, dropping the accent. She was tired of it anyway. "And your reflexes are great. You reacted quickly enough to give Bambi's Scottish cousin plenty of time to get clear. If anyone was at fault, I was, for distracting you."

Josh scowled vaguely at Heather, wondering why she seemed different all of a sudden. Then it hit him. "What happened to the Scottish burr?"

She gave him a twinkling little grin. "I'm afraid I was having a wee bit of fun with you, Josh Campbell."

"So you're not Scottish?"

"Well, I am and I'm not. I was born here, mind you."

He chuckled with quietly amused frustration. The girl couldn't seem to give a straight answer. "Doesn't being born here make you Scottish?"

"That's what I asked my mother," Heather said, laughing. "But Mum brought out the old saw about how a cocker spaniel that happens to be lying in a cold oven when she has her babies is the mother of puppies, not muffins."

"So what's your story, Muffin?" Josh asked.

Heather grinned. She liked the nickname. She liked Josh Campbell. Even if he wasn't The One. "My folks are American," she explained. "Both of them born and raised in the States, their parents Scottish emigrants. From the day Mum and Dad got married, they've traveled all over the world doing their sociological and anthropological studies, writing academic papers and a few popular books, not letting anything stop them—including raising a family. I have three sisters. No two of us claim the same birthplace."

"So that explains the permissiveness," Josh said. "I was sure Scottish parents kept their daughters on a tighter rein." As soon as the comment was out, Josh wished he'd phrased it better. *A tighter rein* was a phrase guaranteed to raise the hackles of any self-respecting American girl.

But to Josh's surprise, Heather merely laughed again, obviously getting a kick out of his remark.

He bristled a little, not used to having a female take everything he said to be funny. "I think I'll talk to your folks about their dereliction of duty. Even if they're busy writing some learned treatise about the Scots of the late twentieth century, they should keep a closer eye on their daughter. There's no excuse for letting you roam alone on remote country roads."

"It's a good thing the road *is* so remote," Heather pointed out. "Given that we're sitting in the middle of it having this long discussion, I mean."

Josh stared at her, realizing with a shock that she was right. What bothered him most was that, with Heather Sinclair sitting beside him, he feared he could have been parked on the Pennsylvania Turnpike at rush hour with no more awareness of his surroundings than he'd had on this lonely Scottish byway.

Clearing his throat, he noticed that he'd turned to lean toward Heather, his arm draped over the back of the car seat. "I'd better get you home," he mumbled, swiveling to face forward, the fingers of both hands curled around the steering wheel. He was horrified by what was happening to him. His taste in women ran to extremely sophisticated types, preferably over thirty. It wasn't like him to be drawn to innocent young girls, and certainly not to flirt with them.

Heather seemed to read his mind. "There's something else I should tell you," she said as he started the car. She'd had enough of letting Josh continue in his mistake about her age—and about her sense of responsibility. "I'm quite a bit older than fifteen. Old enough to live on my own here in Scotland and to run the London and Edinburgh branches of *Dreamweavers*, which is a travel company I own in partnership with my three sisters." She very nearly added, *So there!*, but decided it wouldn't enhance her mature image.

Josh turned to gape at her, then snapped his head back to watch the road. He didn't want any more mishaps. Besides, he was beginning to discover that looking at Heather Sinclair was a bit like drinking too much malt whiskey: It made him dizzy. Especially when she'd thrown him such a curve. "Is this another put-on?" he asked in a low monotone.

Heather smiled with exaggerated sweetness. "I can show you my birth certificate, if you like. Or my baby book, if you need further evidence. I can't let you check with my parents, because they're somewhere in Brazil at the moment. But I assure you, they'd admit I'm all grown up. If it makes you feel any better, I'm the youngest of our family. How about you, Josh? Are you as old as you pretend to be?"

Josh scowled. "What's that remark supposed to mean?"

"I don't know. I just get the impression that you're about thirty going on a hundred." Heather bit down on her lower lip, wishing she hadn't been so blunt.

Josh was taken aback by Heather's powers of observation. For the past few months, he'd felt as if he were a hundred trying to work his way back to thirty.

"Josh, I suspect I've spoken out of turn," Heather said quietly, breaking into his thoughts. "I sometimes blurt out things and wish I could call them back."

"You didn't speak out of turn," Josh said, reaching over to pat Heather's hand, hardly aware of what he was doing until the brief contact sent tiny sparks of heat through his fingers. He pulled back his hand as if recoiling from a shock.

He couldn't understand what was happening. For weeks he'd been like a car with a dead battery, everything in place and no power to draw on. Suddenly, without warning, his inner being seemed to have been jump-started. But how? Why? There was something almost ominous about the abrupt change that had begun to take hold of him from the moment Heather Sinclair had appeared out of the misty rain in front of his car.

For the first time since the needless accident that had turned his existence upside down, he was fully, excitingly, electrically alive.

Two

Josh couldn't help laughing when he saw Heather's neighborhood. "You told me you lived right by the sea, but this is unbelievable," he said as he drove past the unbroken row of structures hugging the Firth of Forth coast. "Town houses that rise straight up out of the ocean? I have to admit, they suit you. They look as if they were erected by the Water Sprite Construction Company."

"Aren't they something?" Heather said with a chuckle, remembering how amazed she'd been the first time she'd laid eyes on the buildings. "In a way, they do rise right out of the ocean. The backs of the houses actually form the seawall. The people who own these places are responsible for keeping their part of the wall in good repair."

"Don't they have flooding problems?" Josh asked. "In a severe storm, for instance?"

Heather gave a little shrug. "From time to time, yes. But it makes no difference. These cottages are always in demand. I guess eccentric charm overrides the occasional inconvenience, like finding an arm of the North Sea decorating your living room."

"How old are they?" Josh asked, utterly fascinated.

"Three, perhaps four centuries. Each neighbor I ask gives me a different vintage." Heather pointed straight ahead toward a parking lot at the end of the street. "You can pull in there," she said. "To answer your earlier question, I do live here by myself, but my cottage isn't on the ocean. It's on the other side of the street."

Josh drew to a stop and switched off the ignition, then turned to peer through the car's back window at the row of buildings tucked into the hillside. "Those places are just as strange as the ones on the waterfront," he remarked with a bemused smile. "They look like oversize blocks pushed into a clay mountain by a petulant baby giant."

Heather arched one delicate brow and grinned. "And you think I talk a lot of foolishness?"

With a shake of his head, Josh sighed. "It must be catching."

Suddenly, Heather felt bereft. She hated to say good-bye to Josh Campbell, not knowing whether she would ever see him again, though as she studiously folded her paisley shawl, she told herself her feelings made no sense. He wasn't the man of her dreams by any standard of measure—though at the moment, she wasn't quite sure why.

Besides, she had to get away from Josh before he saw what a mess she'd made of her feet. He already thought she was slightly idiotic. Why show him any more evidence? What she couldn't decide was whether it would be worse to put on her sandals or negotiate the stone path to her cottage barefoot. She opted for the latter. "Well, thanks again for the ride," she said with forced brightness, reaching for the door handle with one hand, grabbing her shoes with the other.

To his surprise, Josh found that he wasn't ready to let Heather go. He couldn't remember when he'd enjoyed anything as much as the too-short drive with her, no matter how awkward the silences had been at certain moments. "Here, let me play the proper gentleman," he said, jumping out of the car and bounding around to her side. In the brief moment the gesture afforded him to think, he decided to ask her out for dinner.

It was a crazy thing to consider doing, he told himself. Heather Sinclair wasn't his type. Whatever her age, she was too young and innocent for the likes of him. He'd been careful all his life to choose the kind of woman he wasn't likely to hurt, the kind who played by the same rules he did.

Yet to say good-bye to Heather at this moment, without any plans for seeing her again, seemed unthinkable.

While Heather waited for Josh to open the car door, she concentrated on masking any discomfort she might feel when she stood up. She didn't want to leave him with the mental picture of a girl limping home thanks to her own lack of forethought. Pasting on a smile as Josh opened the car door, she swung her body around and braced herself to stand up.

But he glanced down just as she was about to touch ground. "What's that?" he asked, kneeling. "You're bleeding!"

"It's nothing," Heather said hastily, dropping her shoes to the floor of the car as she pulled back her feet and gave in to the childish impulse to try to pull the hem of her skirt over them. "I have a couple of blisters. It's no big deal."

"No big deal?" Josh repeated, grasping both her ankles in his strong, warm hands to raise her feet so he could examine them. "You're a mess, Heather." He looked up at her, shaking his head. "Why would you sit there suffering in silence? I have a first-aid kit in the car; I could've fixed you up in no time."

The combination of irritation and tenderness in his voice shook Heather almost as much as the electricity of his touch. Suddenly she felt extremely vulnerable, an unfamiliar sensation for her—and one she wasn't sure she liked. "I'm fine," she said, amazed to hear a breathless catch in her voice. She tried to tug her feet out of Josh's grip. Being somewhat attracted to the man wasn't entirely puzzling, but the pulse-racing and heart-pounding he seemed to inspire didn't make sense, and certainly didn't fit into the blueprints of her life. "Really, Josh, it looks worse than it is. I'll just go in—"

"You'll just nothing," he said, unexpectedly bending down to sweep her up in his arms. "Now, which house did you say is yours?"

"Josh, you can't carry me!" Heather protested, her cheeks burning, her heart beginning to beat wildly. "I'm not exactly your average featherweight!"

He grinned and arched one heavy blond brow as he kicked the car door shut behind him. "I know. So hurry up and point me to your door before I collapse or drop you." Josh was only half-kidding. Normally, he would have no trouble handling the burden of even a tall, healthy female like Heather, but because his body had been shattered a few months back, he wasn't sure how long his strength would hold up.

Realizing she was in the powerful arms of a man whose will was at least as determined as her own, Heather laughed resignedly and twined her arms around his neck. "I live in the third house down," she told him, indicating the direction by nodding.

"Which number?" he asked as he started toward the place.

"These places don't have numbers," Heather answered, wondering about the throbbing of Josh's heart. Was the unexpected intimacy of the moment affecting him too? Or was she just too heavy for him? "They have names," she went on, a bit shakily. "I live in Maitland Cottage. It's the one with nothing but geraniums in the window boxes. They're the only flowers I can keep healthy, for some reason. I haven't much of a green thumb."

Josh was beginning to think he was in pretty fair shape after all. Heather wasn't a burden. Carrying her, in fact, was giving him acute pleasure. She was soft and womanly, yet very taut, very strong. His libido began responding with alarming enthusiasm. "Why is it called Maitland Cottage?" he asked, trying to converse lightly despite the headiness of the power he suddenly had at his command, the intoxication of Heather's sweet fragrance, the pleasure of her full breasts pressing against his chest. He hadn't been prepared for the onslaught of sensual excitement that suddenly gripped him.

"There's probably some mundane reason, like the first tenant having been named Maitland," Heather said in a small voice. She was in a state of shock, battered by waves of sensation as powerful and mesmerizing as the ocean's rhythmic pounding against the seawall houses.

The tension in her body was transmitted to Josh, stopping him in his tracks as he looked into the evergreen of her eyes. For the first time, he saw no merriment there, no teasing glints that warned of some nonsense to come. To his utter amazement and pleasure, he saw desire. But he also saw confusion. As much confusion as he himself felt.

His arms tightened around Heather. His gaze focused on her slightly parted, inviting lips. His body began remembering demands it had made before it had gone into limbo, along with his entire existence.

"Do you know that you have Loch Ness eyes?" Heather blurted softly, startled by the certainty that Josh was about to kiss her. She was afraid of his kiss. She wanted it too much. She wasn't supposed to want it.

Josh's mouth twitched with a tiny grin. "What are Loch Ness eyes, Heather Sinclair?"

"Bottomless," Heather answered, then couldn't help adding, "with monsters in their depths."

Josh was taken aback. "What if I don't believe in monsters?"

"Just because you don't believe in them doesn't mean they don't exist," Heather answered, surprised at her own words. For all her straightforwardness, she usually managed to be more tactful.

Josh stared at her, not sure how to respond. All of a sudden, Heather seemed anything but young and innocent. Her wisdom and vision were disconcerting. "Do monsters frighten you?" he finally asked, filled with a crazy hope that his inner demons wouldn't faze this woman.

Heather wagged her head slowly from side to side, her self-confidence returning as the moment of intense intimacy seemed to pass, replaced by an intuitive sense that Josh, for all his strength, needed some kind of reassurance. "Do they frighten me?" she repeated. "I don't think so. Monsters are like ghosts in the attic: They're only as scary as we allow them to be. And usually the reason they're hiding in secret places is that they're more frightened than we are."

Josh gazed at Heather for several seconds more, beginning to think she somehow knew him far better than he knew himself. "I don't think I understand this conversation," he murmured at last.

"I'm not sure I do, either," Heather said, then laughed quietly. "But your arms are going to break if you stand here much longer."

Grinning, Josh started walking again. He felt stronger than he had in months. He was in no hurry to relinquish his delectable armful of femininity.

When they reached her door, Heather felt an irrational pang of regret. Despite her moment of panic when a kiss had seemed imminent, she did enjoy being in Josh's arms. "You'd better put me down now," she told him, suppressing a sigh.

"Fish your key from your pocket, unlock your door, and I'll manage," Josh said firmly. "You're not walking on those feet until they're fixed up, understand?" He became aware of another problem. "What's more, you'll be lucky if you don't come down with a chill. Your clothes are damp from the rain. I hope these old houses have modern plumbing, because you need to have a long soak in a hot bath."

"I might just do that," Heather said, pleased that Josh seemed to be in no great hurry to deposit her at her door and leave. "By the way, watch your head and your step," she warned him. "These low doorways weren't built for the likes of you, and there are stairs inside leading down into the house, not up, the way you'd expect."

"Are you going to unlock the door?" he asked.

"There's no need," Heather answered. "I didn't lock it in the first place. It would seem unneighborly." She reached down with one hand to push open the door. "Now remember . . ."

"I know, watch my head and my step," Josh said with exaggerated patience, carefully carrying her through the low, narrow doorway. "I'm more inclined to think I should watch you, young lady. Or someone ought to. You don't lock your door, you go rambling off into the countryside and get yourself lost, you consort with creatures from another dimension—" He stopped as he looked around.

Expecting the interior to be gloomy, Josh was pleasantly surprised by the cheerfulness of the parlor, which he could see through the wide archway to the left of the small entry area. Reflecting the light from the late afternoon sun that streamed through the windows, the room's ivory walls formed a perfect backdrop for groupings of attractively framed paintings and photographs. The floral slipcovers on the couch and chairs, echoed by vases of casual bouquets placed about the room, made for the joyous effect of a country garden.

Drawing a deep breath, Josh inhaled a fragrance of polished wood mingled with the perfume of wildflowers and the elusive whiskey scent of a peat-burning fireplace.

Heather's home sharpened Josh's increasing awareness that she was anything but the young girl he'd first mistaken her for. A woman—not a girl—had created this haven of feminine charm where a man could feel comfortable, a cozy spot that invited him to settle in and put his feet up.

He cleared his suddenly constricted throat. "Where's the bath?"

Heather stared at him, wondering with slight

alarm just what he was planning. "The second door to the right," she answered with a wary frown.

Josh carried her to the bathroom, carefully set her on a low, ladder-backed chair beside the claw-footed tub, then straightened up, trying to convince himself that his heart was pounding because the unaccustomed exertion of the past few minutes had caught up with him. His lips curved in a little smile as his glance took in the blossom-sprigged paper on the walls. "I get the impression you like flowers," he remarked.

"A wee bit," Heather said, struggling to control her labored breathing. "But then, with a name like mine, what could you expect?"

"Should I get the first-aid kit from my car, or do you have one?" he asked, not meeting Heather's eyes.

"I have one," she answered. "It's in that medicine cabinet over the sink."

Josh took the kit from the cabinet, checked to make sure it had everything he felt would be needed, then gave a businesslike little nod. "After you've had your bath, you call me, and I'll come back and take you out to the couch to tend to your feet." Looking around the pleasantly spacious bathroom, he noticed a pale peach terry-cloth robe hanging on a hook on the back of the door. Oddly pleased that there was only the one robe—and that there were no other signs of a male companion—he took it down and handed it to Heather, then leaned over to start running her bath. "Do you want me to put in some of these things?" he asked, picking up the jar of bath beads he found on a small shelf over the bathtub.

As she heard the strain in Josh's voice, Heather realized that he was even more unnerved by the situation than she was. She smiled. "That would be nice," she answered softly.

He sprinkled in the bright pink beads and watched studiously as they bubbled up, releasing a sweet fragrance into the room. "I hope the perfume won't sting your feet," he said as he turned off the tap. He had no idea what it was about Heather that was arousing such protective instincts in him, but he couldn't seem to fight them.

"I'll be fine," Heather said, beginning to enjoy being so coddled.

"Well, you soak as long as you like," Josh said, amazed at how awkward, even shy, he was feeling. "I'll go wait in the living room."

Heather thought she probably ought to tell him she could doctor herself, but somehow she couldn't seem to get the words out. "Thank you," she said instead. "Could I persuade you to have a wee dram while you're waiting?"

"A wee dram?" Josh repeated, then smiled. "It's funny how much more inviting that sounds than a highball or a cocktail or even one-for-the-road."

Heather laughed quietly. "How true. But the Scots are past masters at making things sound cozy. Anyway, if you go into the kitchen and look in the cupboard to the left of the sink, you'll find some good malt whiskey my father bought when he and Mum last visited. I think there's a bottle of Drambuie too. Help yourself to whatever you like."

"I believe I'll do that," Josh said, musing that a bit of Scotch might calm him down. The way his pulse was racing and the blood was heating in his veins, he certainly needed something. What was this enchantress doing to him? "Now make sure you call me as soon as you've finished your bath," he told Heather as he picked up the first-aid kit to take with him. "Don't go walking around on those sore feet."

"Yes, *sir*," Heather said with a teasing grin.

"Would you like a wee dram yourself?" he asked.

She shook her head. She didn't need any more heady influences than Josh Campbell himself was providing.

"How about some tea?"

"Tea would be lovely," Heather answered. "You'll find it right on the cupboard in a canister. I should warn you, I don't have tea bags. I use the loose kind."

"So you can read fortunes in the leaves, no doubt."

"Naturally," Heather said with a grin, though for some reason Josh's mention of fortune-telling bothered her. "Now, there's a little silver tea ball hanging on a hook just above the canister," she went on, firmly refusing to permit old fears to spoil her enjoyment of Josh's attentions. "What you have to do is . . . Oh dear, maybe you shouldn't bother. I really don't need any tea."

Josh gave her an offended look. "I can find my way around a kitchen. And it happens that I was instructed how to make tea properly when I first arrived in Scotland. You just relax, all right?"

"Okay," Heather said as he left, her spirits flagging a little. Teaching a man to make tea involved a special kind of intimacy. Who had given Josh his lessons? How long ago? Maybe the troubled undercurrent she sensed in him stemmed from a tea lady who had captured his heart only to dash it to bits.

It hit Heather that she knew almost nothing about Josh, including whether he was a visitor or actually lived in Edinburgh, and more importantly, whether he was spoken for. And here she was, lounging in her bathtub with him just a couple of rooms away!

Of course his status shouldn't matter to her, she remembered. She wasn't quite twenty-four, so she intended to remain fancy-free for some time to come. And how often, she impatiently asked herself, was she going to need the reminder that Josh Campbell wasn't the least bit like the man she was certain she would recognize at first glance as The Right One?

Nevertheless, Heather decided, she would have to correct her oversight at the very first opportunity. Under the circumstances, it would seem almost indecent not to find out whether Josh had a wife.

Josh peered at the name on the lower right hand corner of each of the whimsical watercolors on Heather's wall. Sipping his Scotch, he stood back and took another look at the paintings. They were her own work, he thought, impressed and amused, but not surprised.

Heather had created a miniature world populated by Cupid-like water babies perched on lily pads, fairy princesses decked out in pale gossamer gowns, gnomes lounging on pastel toadstools, butterflies flexing spun gold wings, and fuzzy caterpillars as appealing as Persian kittens.

And every single creature conveyed a look of sheer joy spiced with a generous helping of incipient mischief. Even Heather's fairy princesses held a promise of impishness in place of the usual passive, dreamy, waiting-for-the-handsome-prince expression.

Smiling, Josh moved on to look at the grouping of photographs he'd noticed earlier. It wasn't long before he'd picked out Heather at various stages of her life, and he wondered as he studied the adolescent girl how he could have underestimated her age by so much.

Perhaps he'd wanted to, he thought. But he chose not to explore that idea any further.

One picture captured his attention more than the others. Taken on the deck of a large sailboat, the name *Dreamweaver* painted in large, clear lettering on the vessel's sparkling white hull, the photograph was an enlarged color snapshot of Heather and three other girls, all of them laughing as they huddled together to look into the camera.

It seemed logical to assume that the boat had inspired the name of the company Heather had mentioned she and her sisters owned, and that the girls with her in the picture were those very sisters. Tall, pretty, so vivacious their liveliness seemed to crackle right out of the snapshot, the Sinclair girls were a fascinating group. Heather, at perhaps sixteen, closely resembled only one of her older sisters, another redhead with a similar tumble of curls, though in more of a light strawberry shade than a russet-gold like Heather's. The other two girls were honey blonds, one with slightly wavy hair, one with a smooth, straight fall that suddenly made him glance back at Heather's paintings.

He began comparing her fantasy creatures with the girls in the various photographs. It was uncanny, he thought, how much he could learn about each of them from the playful way Heather had used them as models and inspiration. He found himself beginning to like this crew of lovely females, wishing he could meet them in person.

The parents, too, seemed interesting—or at least

the couple that had posed with the girls in another photograph and certainly looked like the father and mother of the brood. The older woman was as lovely as her daughters, her eyes merry and expressive like Heather's, while the father's expression suggested the kind of affectionate, long-suffering amusement of a man surrounded by more full-blown femininity than most males could handle.

Having lived most of his own life in almost exclusively male company, Josh wondered with an unexpected little pang of longing what it must be like to be part of a female menagerie.

As he moved back and forth between the photos and the paintings, captivated by Heather's talent, her subtle sense of humor and her obvious affection for her family, he noticed that she'd turned the adjoining dining room into a makeshift studio, complete with an easel on which rested a half-finished work. He stopped in his tracks the moment he went through the old-fashioned archway into the room.

Propped up on the wainscoting halfway up the wall were several sketches. All of men.

Shocked by the tension that suddenly gripped him, Josh made himself move closer to the sketches for a better look.

The knot in his stomach tightened as he saw that Heather had used two models, sketching them from different angles. It was clear that she admired the men; they looked strong and ruggedly handsome, and even in these obviously roughed-out drawings the force of their personalities came through. Josh's eyes narrowed as he studied the dark, piercing eyes of the one man, the crooked grin and roguish expression of the other.

But it was the work on the easel that made

Josh's fingers tighten around his glass. Heather had started a watercolor portrait, using both a pencil drawing for reference and a photograph she'd set up on the wainscoting nearby. The subject was yet a third man, this one dark-haired and good-looking, and to judge by the snapshot, very fond of Heather, as evidenced by the way he was grinning across the table at her, his eyes as brilliant a blue as the azure sea in the background.

If Josh hadn't known he was immune, he'd have thought the emotion wreaking havoc within him was jealousy. But no woman had ever inspired jealousy in him. No woman ever would. He'd seen his father suffer that particular folly. The lesson had been well learned.

Josh was tempted to walk out of Heather Sinclair's house—and her life—before he found himself afflicted with any further maladies. Only his promise to tend her wounds kept him from bolting.

He intended, however, to make his escape the minute he'd fulfilled that promise. The appealing redhead lounging in a bubble bath just a room away wasn't for him.

Three

"I'm all set," Heather called cheerfully from the bathroom.

Josh glanced one more time at the portraits of the men in Heather's life, put down his glass with a sharp rap, and stalked back to her.

He'd reached the bathroom door before he realized what an idiot he was being. What did it matter to him if there were men in Heather Sinclair's life? "Are you decent?" he asked as an excuse to pause long enough to pull himself together.

"Of course," she said with her seductive, husky laugh. "I wouldn't have called you otherwise. But I feel silly."

He took a deep breath and went into the small room. "Why do you feel sil—" His throat closed over. He couldn't finish the word. Heather's pale skin was tinged with pink, her eyes more sparkling than ever, her lips more tempting. And as he gazed at her, knowing she was naked and soft and fragrant under her thick, floor-length robe, he was assaulted by a desire more intense than any he'd ever experienced. And what was worse, it was accompanied by an urge to lift her off the chair just to hold her. To cuddle her, of all things, with quiet tenderness.

Panic began setting in. Cuddle a woman? Tenderly? Not Josh Campbell, he told himself. Josh Campbell didn't have those kinds of impulses toward any woman. "The tea's made," he mumbled. "It should be well steeped by now."

"Thank you," Heather said, wishing she knew what was going on inside Josh. The expression in his eyes when he'd walked into the room had made her whole body go weak, but he'd closed down so quickly, she almost wondered if it had been wishful thinking on her part—which wouldn't make sense anyway, she reminded herself. She didn't want him to look at her in a way that made her go weak.

But when he swept her up in his arms, it was all she could do not to nuzzle her face into the corded warmth of his throat as he carried her to the living room. "You're a nice man," she said softly.

Lowering her to one end of the chintz-covered couch in a half-sitting position, Josh found it difficult to release her. Even when he did manage to pull away, he was captivated by the way she looked against the bold backdrop of daisies, pink cabbage roses, and lily of the valley, like one of her imaginary fairy people peeking out at him from under a leaf in the midst of a patch of flowers.

He gave himself a mental shake, annoyed that he was becoming almost as ridiculously fanciful as Heather herself. "You shouldn't jump to that kind of conclusion about anyone on such flimsy evidence," he said as he looked down at her. "I'm not a nice man, Heather. Believe me. Especially where vulnerable young ladies like you are concerned."

Heather stared at Josh, wondering what had brought on that heated denial. Finally, she spoke very quietly. "I should believe you. Common sense tells me to believe you. People rarely describe themselves more harshly than they deserve. But, Josh, I'm afraid I can't accept what you're trying to say. So let's just leave it at this: Whatever your dark side might be, from what I've seen of you, you're a nice man."

Josh decided there wasn't much point trying to argue, but he was more convinced than ever that he had to nip this mutual attraction in the bud. He would get Heather's tea, fix up her cuts and blisters, make sure she had a bite to eat, and be on his way. The sooner the better. He turned on his heel and strode out to the kitchen.

Heather was disconcerted. Josh seemed determined that she wouldn't think too highly of him, yet everything he did was so thoughtful and sweet, she couldn't do otherwise.

She wondered if she ought to offer him dinner—just by way of thanks, she told herself hastily. But she had almost nothing in her pantry beyond basics and a few vegetables.

All at once an inspiration hit her. She could call her neighbor. Annie MacLean would have something in her well-stocked freezer.

Heather reached for the phone on the table at the end of the couch and dialed Annie's number. There was no answer, and Heather was surprised at how disappointed she felt at knowing she had only a few minutes to spend with Josh.

Just as he was returning from the kitchen with the tea tray, there was a knock at her door. Calmly, he put the tray on the table in front of the couch, went to the door, and opened it.

"Oh, my goodness me," Heather heard.

Her mood lifted instantly as she laughed at the awed sound of her friend's voice. "Come in, Annie," she called, noting that Fate was being strangely cooperative when Josh wasn't remotely suitable as a candidate for The One And Only. "This is Josh Campbell," Heather said to Annie, wondering why the woman kept staring at Josh as if seeing an apparition. "Josh, meet my next-door neighbor, Annie MacLean."

"Pleased to meet you," Josh said politely, stepping back as the diminutive brunette in a red plaid shirt and snug jeans entered the cottage. He didn't try to shake hands with her; she was holding a large, foil-wrapped package.

"Rob brought home a fresh salmon from his fishin' trip up to the old family croft," Annie said, her brown eyes huge and round as she kept gaping at Josh. "There's too much for us, so I thought you might like some, Heather. It's all cleaned and filleted, ready for cookin'." At last Annie dragged her gaze from Josh and looked at Heather, her forehead creasing in a frown. "But what's wrong with you, lass? Are you ill?"

"I'm fine," Heather said, smiling broadly. Salmon fresh from a Highland stream ought to tempt Josh. "And you and Rob are a pair of angels. I'll try to do something just as nice for you one of these days."

"Och, never mind. You do nice things for us all the time. Now, tell me what you've gone and done to yourself this time."

Heather hoped that Josh hadn't noticed Annie's last two words. There was no need for him to know that she was often a bit of a klutz. "I walked too far without proper shoes and got some blisters, that's all," she answered. "Josh rode to the rescue, then insisted on coming in to doctor my feet. But we were about to have some tea. Will you stay for a cup, Annie?"

"I believe I could spare a few minutes," the petite woman answered. "The salmon should be put in the refrigerator, though." She turned to Josh and smiled sweetly.

It took him a couple of seconds to get the hint. "I'll put it away," he said, taking it from her. "And I'll get another cup at the same time."

"Och, that'd be lovely," Annie said, beaming at him all too brightly. The instant Josh was gone, she descended on Heather. "It's *him*!" she whispered.

"Him?" Heather repeated. "Who?"

"The fair-haired giant of a man who was in my dream last night. An *American*, just like this lad!"

Heather grinned. "Well, I'll admit that Josh is the stuff of dreams, but shame on you, Annie. You with a wonderful husband like Rob—"

"It was *you* with him," Annie interrupted. "He walked right into your house, picked you up, threw you over his shoulder like a sack of oats, and carried you off."

Heather chuckled. "I'd like to see him try. Big as he is, I've a few tricks up my sleeve." This confirmation of her mental picture of a Viking abduction appealed to her sense of drama, however, so she encouraged Annie to go on with the tale. "Where did he carry me off to?" she asked eagerly.

Annie's eyes grew even bigger. "I've no idea, lass. In my dream, you yourself didn't know where he was takin' you, and all the kickin' and hollerin' you did was to no avail."

"Well, it won't happen," Heather said with a

complacent smile that masked the resurgence of her earlier nagging fear. Still unable to pin down the fleeting recollection that was the source of her discomfort, she blamed her foolish anxiety on the fact that Annie's dreams were notorious for coming true. But this one was ridiculous, Heather decided. It was a funny coincidence, nothing more. "Much as I loved my gypsy childhood," she went on with a show of bravado, "I made up my mind very early in life that when I was grown up, nobody but Heather Sinclair would decide where, when, why, and how I went anywhere. And with whom, I might add." She grinned as a thought struck her. "How do you know Josh is an American?"

Annie raised her brows in obvious surprise. "Why, by his accent, of course."

"Of course," Heather said with a quiet chuckle. She'd traveled a great deal in her life, and one thing she'd observed was that people always thought everyone *else* had an accent. "Do you have any idea what a lifesaver you are, Annie?" she asked in a low voice. "Just before you knocked, I was trying to call you because I wanted to invite Josh to stay for dinner but hadn't anything to feed him."

"You'll be wantin' more than the fish, though there's plenty of salmon for two," Annie said, her curiosity and superstition displaced by the concerns of her practical side. "I'll go home and see what I can put together—"

"No, it's fine," Heather interrupted. "I have rice, there are vegetables in the garden, and there's even some ice cream in the freezer for dessert. All I need now is to persuade Josh to stay." And to answer a few questions, she added silently. Such as whether there was a Mrs. Josh. Such as who had taught him to make a good *cuppa* using loose tea leaves. Such as why Heather Sinclair was thinking one way and acting another.

"Listen, my girl," Annie said, glancing toward the kitchen door to be sure Josh wasn't walking in on the woman-to-woman conversation, "when a man you've just met comes into your house, makes tea for you, and plans to bandage the blisters on your toes, I truly doubt it will be difficult to talk him into sharin' a bit of supper with you. Besides, I know he'll stay. I have a sixth sense about this man and you."

Heather giggled. "Get that look off your face, Annie. I only want to thank Josh for all his kindness. You know he's not The One. My Other Half, when I do find him, will be quiet and gentle, probably a very polished Englishman, a gentleman farmer with a huge manor house full of family ghosts. He'll look perfect in elegant European-cut suits. He'll bring order and security to my life. Josh is just like my three brothers-in-law. I love them all, but I couldn't live with any one of them. You never know what they're going to be up to next, career-wise or otherwise; they're all too big, too bossy, and too . . . too American."

"Aye," Annie said with a roll of her eyes that spoke volumes. "Josh is just the sort who could toss you over his shoulder if he'd a mind to. Listen, Heather Sinclair. You may think you've got this One And Only you keep blatherin' about all ordered up, like a tasty dish at an inn, but you wouldna be the first lass who had it all wrong. And my dream says you do."

"I don't know Josh at all," Heather argued, extremely unsettled by Annie's remarks, and not prepared to examine why. "He might not even be single."

Annie rolled her eyes again to show that her patience was being sorely tried. "If that lovely fellow belonged to you, lass, would you let him out of your sight?"

Heather thought about the question for a few seconds, then laughed. "I'd nail his boots to the floor first," she admitted.

"So would any female with half a brain," Annie said with a nod of triumph. "And your Josh has a way about him that's . . . well, I can't explain except to say he doesn't have the look of a married man." As Josh's footsteps warned of his approach, Annie added in a low whisper, "Trust me, he strikes me as a man worth considerin'." She winked. "Even if he *is* a Campbell!"

Annie left after only a few minutes, downing her tea in record time, and Josh decided it was time to discharge his duties so he could be on his way. After lowering himself to the end of the couch, he slid one of his large hands under Heather's calves and carefully positioned her legs so her feet were extending just beyond his lap. "This house is really something," he said, reaching for the first-aid kit he'd put on the end table earlier. Small talk, he'd decided, would help him get past this intimate moment. He opened the medicine box and took out a bottle of lotion and a paper-covered square of cotton gauze, then put the kit on Heather's lap where it would be handy to get at. "I've never seen a kitchen that looked about two stories high and had a stairway up the side of it," he went on. "Where do the stairs lead?"

"To the garden," Heather answered absently, wondering if she could assume Josh was unencumbered because he wore no ring.

"There's a garden *above* your kitchen?" he asked, ripping open the packet of gauze.

"That's right," Heather said. "The kitchen is in the part of the house that's pushed into the side of the hill, so the garden on the hill is on the roof of the kitchen."

Josh opened two more gauze packets when he saw how many cuts and blisters Heather had. "How did you end up with this place?" he asked, firmly resisting another wave of tender protectiveness that was tugging at him.

"Some friends from my University of Edinburgh days rented it to me. They live in an apartment in the heart of the city because it's more convenient for them, but when they inherited this cottage, they didn't want to sell it. They knew I was looking for a place, so they called and told me about it."

Josh couldn't help chuckling. "I can't imagine why they'd think of you for an offbeat house like this." He was quiet for a moment, but the silence suddenly seemed charged again with an underlying excitement. It had to be dispelled. He cleared his throat. "How did you happen to go to the University of Edinburgh?" he asked with forced casualness.

"For several reasons," Heather said, glad Josh had cut into the tension she'd felt building between them. But she wondered how he'd managed to turn things around so he was getting answers and she wasn't. "Mainly because I enjoy this city so much. And the university is first-rate. I majored in history, so Edinburgh seemed like a logical choice for me." Enough, she decided. It was her turn. "How long have you been in Scotland, Josh?"

"About eighteen months," he answered.

"In Edinburgh?"

"Ten months in Edinburgh. Eight in the Shetland Islands," he said tersely.

Something in Josh's tone made her proceed carefully. "You're involved in the oil industry, then?"

Josh nodded. "I was."

"Past tense?"

"Very past tense." Josh gave Heather a rather unconvincing smile, then took the cap off the lotion bottle. "What have you done to yourself? Not only do you have blisters and cuts, you look as if you've done the Highland Fling on a field of burdocks and Scottish thistles."

Heather frowned. Was he being evasive? She decided to try a roundabout approach to the question of his availability. His very elusiveness fired Heather's determination to pry an answer out of the man. "You were right about knowing how to make wonderful tea. Where on earth did you learn?"

"From a cook on the oil rig," Josh answered. "And it isn't such an amazing skill. In fact, I actually know several men who've mastered the technique, believe it or not."

Heather laughed, both from amusement and from pleasure at learning that there didn't seem to be a tea lady in Josh's background. Encouraged, she tried another gambit. "Am I keeping you from anything?" she asked with a look of innocence.

"Not that I know of," Josh said, clicking his tongue as he surveyed the damage to her feet. He took a pair of tweezers from the first-aid kit and began pulling out the thistles that were imbedded in the bottoms of her feet. "What were you trying to prove by keeping your misery to yourself, anyway? Where is it written you have to be such a stoic?"

"Complaining doesn't lessen the misery, does it?" Heather said, scowling slightly. "I was grateful not to have to walk any farther; I didn't see the sense in crying about a few scratches when nothing could be done about them. How was I to know you had a first-aid kit in your car?"

Josh said nothing as he tipped some antiseptic lotion onto the gauze square, daubed carefully at the patches her sandal straps had rubbed raw, then tended to the broken blisters. For some reason it bothered him to think of hurting her, even for her own good. "I hope this stuff is the kind that doesn't sting," he murmured.

"It doesn't," Heather said. "I don't suffer pain willingly." She hesitated, then asked as casually as possible, "Are you expected at home at a certain hour?" Surely a question like that would make him tell her if he had a wife waiting for him, she thought.

"No," he answered, shaking his head at an especially nasty cut she'd somehow managed to get. "Tell me, Heather, if you don't suffer pain willingly, how do you explain going off on a major hike wearing sandals?"

"It wasn't such a major hike," she protested, beginning to get a little impatient with his scolding. "It wasn't as if I was trying to climb Ben Nevis or some such thing. And since I had meant to take buses for most of my outing, I thought sandals would be fine. Besides, I'm sure our ancestors roamed these Highlands without benefit of Reeboks."

"But their feet were calloused enough to take the punishment," Josh pointed out. "Yours are too soft to be treated to the harsh kiss of a Scottish thistle." His thumb grazed the silken underside of her arch. "Much too soft," he added just above a whisper.

The sudden, caressing note in his voice sent a shiver through Heather's whole body, making her forget to be even a little irritated. And his touch was so mesmerizingly gentle, she was tempted to point to a few imaginary wounds just to have him tend them.

But how could she respond to him with such excitement when she couldn't seem to find out something as basic as his marital status? She was shocked at herself. And was Josh ducking the issue? His answers certainly did leave a little something to be desired.

As Josh began applying bandages to the worst wounds, Heather made another stab at learning a few basic facts about him. "Do you have an apartment in Edinburgh?"

He nodded, concentrating on what he was doing.

"Is it a small apartment?" she prompted.

"One bedroom," Josh answered, wrapping a bandage around her baby toe. The gist of Heather's questions finally got through to him. "I live alone," he said, impaling her with a hard, level gaze. "I'm not married. I've never been married. I don't intend to be married in the future. Or to be involved with any one woman. Understand, little girl?"

Heather's eyes flashed. "Who asked you, Campbell?" she shot back, sticking out her chin.

Josh stared at her as he wiped his hands on a piece of gauze, not sure whether to laugh at her justifiable pugnaciousness or teach her a quick lesson in reality.

He decided on the latter. Setting aside the first-aid kit, he lifted Heather's feet from his lap and carefully placed them on the couch cushions, then moved up beside her. "Nobody asked me, Muffin," he said quietly, taking her empty cup and putting it on the coffee table. "But let's be straight with each other. There are some interesting sparks between us, aren't there?"

Heather was too inherently honest to try to deny his claim, but his unexpected display of arrogance irked her. "Sparks don't have to start major conflagrations," she said, then swallowed hard as she saw dangerous golden flames in Josh's eyes and felt the fires of response deep inside herself. She tried to speak, battling the melting sensation that was overtaking her, but she couldn't utter another word.

Josh cradled her face between his hands and bent to brush his lips over hers. "But some sparks do start major conflagrations," he murmured, then toyed with her mouth, deliberately and expertly teasing her until he felt her breathing becoming ragged, her arms twining around his neck, her breasts swelling against his chest. He told himself that Heather needed to learn to be less trusting of men like Josh Campbell. She had to be taught how vulnerable she was.

Heather tried to make herself summon at least some resistance to the drugging effects of Josh's kiss, but her will was paralyzed, overruled by a sudden need such as she'd never dreamed could grip her. She wanted only to feel Josh, to taste him, breathe in his tantalizing male scent, mold her body to his. For an instant that stamped itself indelibly on her very soul, Heather's entire being seemed to merge with the essence that was Josh Campbell. It was the most exciting yet most terrifying moment she'd ever experienced.

And at that same instant in the lesson he'd meant to give, not to receive, Josh realized that something much larger than he had expected or was ready for was happening. As Heather's lips parted and her tongue began making its own eager exploration of his mouth, her body softening against his until the tenderness he'd been battling threatened to overwhelm him completely, he knew he had to grab for his self-control like a drowning man clutching at a lifeline.

In desperation, he wrapped his arms around Heather's slender body, gathering her close to him, the blood pounding in his head, making him dizzy. "Heather," he whispered, releasing her mouth long enough to gaze down at her in utter shock. "What are you doing to me?"

Before she could say anything, he found himself lost to pure sensation once again, capturing Heather's lips, craving the taste of her, the warmth and sweetness. He wanted to believe that the wild need she'd aroused in him was just a fluke of timing, a simple matter of a libido that had been denied too long. But it wasn't true. He wanted Heather. Only Heather.

As his grip on self-control rapidly loosened, he made one last-ditch attempt to save himself. With a supreme act of will, he forced himself to pull back, curving his fingers around Heather's shoulders to hold her at arm's length. "This wasn't supposed to happen!" he said, shocked by the edge of panic in his voice.

Heather simply stared at him in mute agreement. Such a moment had never been meant to happen to her. Not with anyone. Certainly not with this man.

Josh gave her a little shake. "Don't you know better than to throw yourself at a strange male?"

Heather blinked slowly, not sure she'd heard right. "I threw myself at you?" she asked carefully.

"What would you call it?" Josh demanded, fully aware how unreasonable he was being but desperately trying to salvage something from the so-called lesson he'd intended to teach her. "On top of all the other knuckleheaded things you've done today, you've let me kiss you the way . . . the way I just kissed you . . ."

"I do believe you let me kiss you the same way," Heather said, her quiet manner masking the tremors of anger rumbling within her. "Does that make you a knucklehead too?"

Josh took a deep breath and got to his feet. "Yes," he said with low intensity. "Yes, it makes me the worst kind of knucklehead." Unable to look at Heather's full pink mouth and still resist its temptation, Josh turned sharply, intending to put some distance between himself and the couch. As his shin smashed against the edge of the coffee table, he let out a stream of muttered curses.

"Oh dear, that must hurt so much," Heather said, her anger forgotten in her instant concern.

Josh refused to let her sweetness soften him. "Not half as much as you're going to get hurt, young lady, if you don't learn a few simple self-protective devices to help you make your way through a dangerous world with some degree of safety." He hated the way he sounded, like a greenhorn school principal delivering a jargon-loaded lecture, but under the circumstances he couldn't manage anything better.

"You know, you sound just like Cole," Heather said, her forehead creased in a frown. She'd been right in what she'd told Annie. Being attracted to Josh was impossible. He was too much like Cole in every way except his coloring. Cole was wonderful—for Morgan. Not for Morgan's baby sister.

"Who's Cole?" Josh asked. "One of the men

you're immortalizing in that little studio of yours? The guy on the easel?" he asked with a rush of inexplicable anger.

"As a matter of fact, I do plan to do Cole's portrait," Heather said. "But the one on the easel is Pete."

"Pete, is it? And I suppose both those poor saps worry about you? Fuss over you just the way I've been doing?"

Heather scowled. "A little, yes. But that's just the overprotectiveness that men like you and Cole and T.J. and Pete tend to indulge in, whether or not it's invited or welcomed. And I'll thank you not to refer to them as poor saps. They happen to be three of the least sappy men I've ever had the pleasure of encountering."

"Well, apparently you ought to know," Josh muttered, stunned by the fury ripping through him. "All about men, that is. Do these characters know about each other? Is Cole, for instance, aware that he's not your only . . . only portrait subject?"

"He doesn't even know he's a subject," Heather answered, thoroughly confused by the conversation. "I'm trying to paint all my brothers-in-law as a Christmas surprise for my sisters. But what do those portraits have to do with whatever you and I were discussing? If you could call it a discussion, that is."

Josh raked his fingers through his hair and stared down at the floor, wishing he could fall through it. "Nothing," he said after several moments. "Nothing at all." Reaching into his pocket for his car keys, he turned on his heel and headed for the door. "I'd better get out of here. Thanks for the Scotch."

"What's wrong, Josh?" Heather asked, her head spinning from the rapid-fire changes in him.

"Heaven knows, I'm as startled by what you just made me feel as you seem to be, but was it really so terrible of me to respond when you kissed me?"

"Yes!" he shouted, then stopped at the living room archway and turned to face Heather again. "No," he admitted more quietly. "But I don't understand what's going on. I'm a calm, reasonable man who minds his own business and lets others mind theirs. I don't lecture women about how they run their lives. I don't jump to stupid conclusions on flimsy evidence. I don't ask ladies whether there are other men in their lives, because I don't care. I don't do any of the things I've been doing since the first minute I laid eyes on you, Heather Sinclair, and that's why I'm getting out of this place. Because I feel as if you really have put some kind of hex on me, and I don't even believe in such things. So good-bye, good luck, it's been interesting knowing you." This time, refusing to give in to the compulsion to go back to Heather and coax another melting response from her, he forced himself to ascend the small stairway and leave the strange little house.

Heather sat very still as she heard the door close behind Josh. "Wonderful," she murmured disgustedly, grabbing a throw cushion to hug. "I kiss a handsome, sweet prince and turn him into a raging frog."

With a deep sigh, she reminded herself that she'd had no business letting Josh kiss her the way he had, that her faulty memory was exaggerating the totality of her surrender, that it was good riddance to such a moody character, no matter how kind he could be in his better moments.

She told herself that as soon as her heartbeat settled back to normal and her lips stopped tingling and the burning liquid inside her cooled, she would set about the task of forgetting that Josh Campbell existed.

She stuck out her lower lip in a pout. Josh Campbell was the wrong prince anyway. For all she cared, he could go sit on a lily pad and spend the rest of his days growing warts on his nose. Maybe they'd make him less devastatingly attractive to hapless lady frogs who had the misfortune to splash down in his pond.

Four

Josh was halfway to his car when he stopped, turned to frown at Heather's house for several seconds, gave his head a little shake, then continued on his way. Two steps from his car he stopped again, cursed under his breath—and suddenly laughed.

A moment later he was bounding back toward Heather's door, and after three sharp knocks, pushed it open. "Don't get up," he said as soon as he was inside. "It's only me."

Heather was shocked by the lift of her spirits at the mere sound of Josh's voice. And when his large frame filled the parlor archway, her heartbeat went crazy all over again. "Did you forget something?" she managed to ask despite an attack of breathlessness.

Josh remained still, not moving, not speaking. Yes, he thought, he'd forgotten something. He'd forgotten how maddeningly, delectably, dangerously feminine Heather looked reclining on the flower-splashed couch, her high cheekbones flushed pink, her eyes as dark as a wild Highland forest, her soft lips invitingly parted. "The salmon," he muttered at last. "The one Annie brought. You can't very well cook the thing in the shape you're in, so it occurred to me that I'd better come back and do it."

Though Heather was duly grateful for Josh's concern, she was less than thrilled by his grudging manner. "You needn't worry. I can manage," she said, her voice unnaturally high and stilted. "If all else fails, I'll improvise Scottish sushi." Swinging her legs around, she steeled herself to keep her expression impassive as her feet touched the floor. "See?" she said, managing a bright smile. "I'm just fine. I can cope perfectly well without being any further burden on—" She caught her breath as Josh suddenly covered the distance from the entryway to her in two long strides and swept her up in his arms.

"I didn't go to all the trouble of bandaging those blisters so you could mess them up again," he said, his throat constricting as he reeled under the gentle but powerful impact of Heather's intriguing softness. He deposited her rather unceremoniously on the couch. "You just stay right here while I fix dinner," he ordered. He didn't like sounding so brusque, but it was his only line of defense. "If you'll show a grain of sense for a change, you just might be as good as new by morning."

Heather stared up at him, caught in another whirl of confused emotions. Her first reaction was to inform Josh Campbell, with all the hauteur she could summon, that she wasn't accustomed to being picked up and dropped here and there like a garage-sale end table, wasn't used to being spoken to as if she were a silly, difficult child, and didn't need him to play the Galloping Gourmet or anything else.

But as she clutched her robe tightly around her body, Heather found herself sounding more hurt than defiant, and she couldn't seem to help thrusting out her lower lip in a pout. "I've been enough of a nuisance to you already," she said with a sniff. "I'm not all that hungry, so you can just be on your *un*-merry way. Take the salmon home and . . . and stick it in your own oven."

Josh stood gazing down at Heather's alluring mouth, barely managing to keep his primitive urges in check. "You're not a nuisance," he said, suddenly realizing just how gruff he must have sounded—and how idiotically he'd been behaving. With a grin, he added, "At least, you won't be one if you stay put while I get some grub together. Okay, Muffin?"

Heather melted. Instantly and completely. She had no idea why. The reaction went against everything she believed, everything she was. Yet she couldn't seem to fight it. And when Josh went into the kitchen, leaving her alone with her thoughts, she was alarmed by how much the scene of a few minutes earlier had resembled Annie's dream.

She stiffened her backbone. If resisting Josh Campbell meant fighting Fate itself, then Fate was in for a Battle Royal.

During the dinner Josh brought in on trays, Heather found her resolve weakening again. She was drawn to the man no matter how hard she tried not to be.

Her first taste of a succulent morsel of wine-poached salmon signaled trouble. Things weren't going right, she thought. Her Dream Man would be a terrific cook. Not Josh. He didn't suit the part.

He was remarkably charming as he sat in the wing chair across from her, quizzing her with apparently genuine interest about the photographs on the walls. Before she knew what was happening, she was chatting away to Josh as if she had no reason to be wary of him, telling him all about her three sisters, her parents, and the Sinclair family's unorthodox way of life.

"So you actually grew up aboard that sailboat," Josh said, glancing at the picture of the girls on the deck of the vessel that was named the *Dreamweaver*.

Heather nodded. "Also in the various places where my mother and father were doing their studies, usually observing remote cultures that have ignored and been ignored by the twentieth century in varying degrees. I've lived in villages from the Hebrides to South American rain forests to obscure South Sea islands."

"And now, at the tender age of twenty-three, you're here in Edinburgh running the British offices of *Dreamweavers, Inc.*," Josh said with a quizzical smile, getting up from his chair to refill Heather's goblet with the excellent Chablis he'd been pleased to find in her refrigerator. The wine had been a gift, she'd told him, from a client who'd been particularly pleased with the Scottish Border Country vacation she'd organized. "You say your branch of the family firm offers tours of haunted houses, medieval castles, and unexplained ruins from ancient times," Josh said with a teasing grin as he topped up his own glass and sat down again. "Let me guess whose idea that gimmick was."

"You'd guess right," Heather said, laughing. "In fact, as I think I mentioned when you first picked me up, what I was doing before I literally got off on the wrong track today was checking out a possible country walk—our clients seem to like an occasional search for fairies on the hikes we organize, and my friend Maharg told me that Alva Glen is supposed to be a favorite dwelling for the creatures—"

"Do you actually believe the things you say about haunted places and sprites and fairies?" Josh interrupted, at the same time vaguely wondering who this friend Maharg was that Heather kept mentioning.

Heather paused for a moment, deciding whether to answer Josh seriously or tease him a little. She chose to be serious—more or less. "It's hard to spend much time in Scotland without being tempted to believe in such things, just a wee bit." She took a forkful of wild and brown rice, concentrated for a moment on the subtle seasonings Josh had added, then shook her head, still unable to absorb that a man who looked like a slightly battered rodeo cowboy could whip up a meal worthy of a Cordon Bleu graduate.

Josh had another question for her. "Tell me something, Heather: Don't your clients—especially kids—get a bit upset when they don't see any ghosts and fairies on their outings?"

"But they do see them!" Heather answered with great fervor. "It's just like ghost tales told around a campfire. You see, at *Dreamweavers*, we make it clear that our tours are for fun, for a stretch of the imagination, whether we're talking about the pirate cruises my sister Morgan runs in the Caribbean, the riverboat Stefanie operates out of New Orleans, or even the art tours Lisa arranges throughout the south of France. We provide the settings and our customers add their own fantasies, perhaps imagining Van Gogh at his easel in a field of sunflowers near Arles, or pretending to be plying the Mississippi in the time of Mark Twain, or preparing to attack a treasure-laden galleon . . ." Heather grinned. "Or seeing sprites and fairy folk hiding behind every tree, or even headless horsemen, if that's your persuasion. And for the more serious-minded travelers—in other words, those of all ages who don't know how to be kids—we make sure every tour operated by *Dreamweavers* has scenic, historical, and often literary interest."

Thoroughly enjoying the streak of practicality under Heather's frivolous surface, Josh laughed quietly. It was something he'd found himself doing a great deal since he'd first encountered Heather Sinclair. In fact, he'd laughed more in these short hours than he had in a very long time. For months he'd been fighting his way back from helplessness and despair, and with a lot of help, he'd beaten some heavy odds. But he suspected he'd become a pretty grim character in the process.

And never—before or after the disaster—had he felt as alive, excited, and stimulated as he had since this red-haired imp of a girl had leapt out at him on a lonely country road.

As Heather sensed Josh relaxing and even warming to her a little, she couldn't resist trying to satisfy her curiosity about him, starting with his kitchen expertise. She'd begun to wonder again whether some woman—some heartbreaker—lurked in his background, one who had taught him how to cook. Heather did, however, attempt to use a touch more subtlety than she normally managed. "Where did you pick up your gourmet skills?" she asked after she'd heaped compliments on him for the wonderful meal. "Did your mother teach you?"

Josh's expression hardened almost imperceptibly. "My father raised me by himself from the time I was ten. I learned to cook out of sheer self-defense. Pop's idea of feeding a kid a great meal was to send out for a pizza, or if he was feeling really ambitious, to whip up a batch of popcorn and add a side dish of peanut butter sandwiches. It's amazing how quickly a fast-food diet loses its appeal even to a kid when there's no mother on the scene to nag about proper nutrition." After an infinitesimal pause, he went on lightly, "So when the enlightened teachers at my grade school offered one of those role-reversal things, where girls could sign up for woodworking and boys could take a basic cooking course, I was at the head of the line."

Heather wondered what had happened to Josh's mother when he'd been ten. Whatever it had been, he clearly didn't want to talk about it. Curious as Heather was, she respected his desire for privacy.

Despite the amusingly incongruous mental picture of Josh lining up to take culinary classes, her lighthearted mood began to take on a more somber aspect. Realizing that she'd been gazing thoughtfully at him for several moments, she asked, "Were you an only child?"

"I'm the only offspring," Josh said with a wry smile. "I'm not sure I ever was a child." As he heard the harshness in his voice, he decided that his comment was too much like soul-baring for his taste. He was becoming far too comfortable with Heather, too happy in her company. He stood and picked up the trays. "I'll go do the dishes," he muttered, reverting to his brusque manner. He had no right to get involved on any level with a woman like Heather.

Heather was puzzled and slightly dismayed by Josh's sudden switch back to his earlier clipped tones. "Leave the dishes," she said, abruptly deciding that this man was too moody for her taste after all. He might be exciting, but if she was going to allow herself to be attracted to anyone, she intended to make sure he was uncomplicated, open, good-natured, and easygoing. Josh didn't fill her shopping list in any of those particulars. "I can clean up the kitchen in the morning before I go to work," she added. "You've done enough for me as it is."

"It'll only take me a few minutes," Josh said, heading for the kitchen. "And then I'll be on my way."

Heather opened her mouth to protest, but she snapped her jaw shut before she could utter one foolish word. The sooner Josh was gone, the sooner she would be able to sort out her scrambled feelings. Besides, she'd learned that it was pointless to try to talk him out of anything once he'd made up his mind—just like the men her three sisters had married. She wondered if gravitating toward overly strong, complex males was a genetic flaw in the makeup of the Sinclair women.

When Josh returned to the living room, he stood looking at Heather, thinking. Finally he spoke. "I should carry you to your bedroom before I leave."

Heather gave a strained laugh. She wasn't about to allow Josh Campbell to put her to bed, and she could be as stubborn as any male, including this one. "I'm not an invalid, Josh. I do appreciate all your tender care, but I'm fine," she said with a deceptively mild smile. "Honestly, my feet already feel much better. Anyway, I'll probably just sleep right here on the couch tonight. I do that a lot."

"Are you sure?" he asked, at the same time wondering why he would choose to torment himself with the thought of seeing Heather Sinclair lying in bed, looking up at him with those misty green eyes of hers.

"I'm sure," Heather said, proud of how strong and firm she sounded despite the infernal flutters he was able to arouse in her at every turn. "Thank you so much for everything you've done, Josh. You've been more than kind."

Josh knew a dismissal when he heard one. "Glad to be of service," he said tightly.

But he couldn't make himself go. It was as if invisible chains were holding him. "By the way, I noticed that Annie asked you what you'd done to yourself *this* time," he added as a last-ditch measure to cover the awkward moment. "I take it you're in the habit of getting into the kind of situation you were in today?"

Heather had hoped that Josh had overlooked Annie's comment. But she wasn't surprised that he'd noticed it. She suspected that Josh Campbell didn't miss much. "You might say I occasionally tend to forget my limitations," she admitted, suddenly beginning to talk quickly and a great deal, reluctant to see him go. "It started when I was little, always trying to keep up with Morgan and her daring ways. Lisa had the sense not to attempt to be another female Captain Blood like Morgan was, and Stefanie was the oldest, so she didn't feel she had to keep up with anyone, but I couldn't seem to help wanting to show myself and the world at large that anything Morgan did, I could do almost as well. It never worked."

"For instance?" Josh asked, unable to resist prompting Heather to go on for just another moment or two.

Heather laughed. "There were so many for-instances. One time, I remember, our whole family was at a fair on a remote island in the South

Pacific, and I managed to follow Morgan everywhere without her suspecting it. When she tried her hand at some game of chance and won, I waited until she'd moved on and then I tried—and usually lost. When she went to a sort of gypsy booth to have her fortune read, I—" Heather stopped abruptly as a chill seemed to pass through her body, and she found herself shrinking from the memory that had been trying to surface since the first moment she'd laid eyes on Josh. "That's too long a story to get into," she went on hastily, her tone somewhat subdued. "Suffice it to say that even if it was just a matter of my chasing after Morgan through the jungle on one of her imaginary Terry-and-the-Pirates missions, she would end up looking as if she'd been out for a quiet stroll in London's Hyde Park, but you'd swear I'd been mauled by a flock of lovesick parakeets."

Josh chuckled, more intrigued with Heather than ever. But he'd already committed himself to leaving; how could he change his mind? And he couldn't keep standing in the doorway, stalling. He had to go. And in the long run, he kept telling himself, he would be glad he had put an end to this flirtation in its early stages. "Well, try to stay out of those parakeet-infested jungles, Muffin," he said with another forced smile.

Offering a little two-fingered salute, he made his getaway before he could change his mind and do something as knuckleheaded as going to Heather Sinclair and hauling her into his arms for another unforgettable, heart-jolting kiss.

And when he'd gone, Heather felt alone in a way she couldn't remember ever feeling before.

Josh reached across the Austin's passenger side to open the car door. "Hop in, Maggie," he said when Margaret Alexander dashed from the clinic's entrance through the rain.

"I can't believe I forgot my umbrella!" Maggie said in her quiet lilt, laughing and settling into the seat, putting her handbag on the floor in front of her. "It's a good thing I love the rain."

"That's why you ran so hard to get out of it," Josh said with teasing affection as he maneuvered the car into the busy early-evening traffic.

"I just didn't want to get the seat all wet," Maggie shot back. "You're as besotted with cars as Donald is, and I know how he hates seeing the leather interior of his precious little Lotus get even a bit damp. Sometimes I'm tempted to wrap my sweet husband's steering wheel around his neck, I swear. He's *such* a fussbudget. How was your checkup?"

Josh smiled. He was used to Maggie's meaningless, good-natured complaints about her husband, as well as to her quick subject changes. "Great, thanks to you and Donald," he answered. "The doctor told me that the feats of strength Donald's been pushing me to do have been the perfect supplement to the tortures you used to put me through at the clinic. I can get back to work anytime, it seems—as long as I don't return to deep-sea diving. All I have to do now is figure out what my new career is going to be." Josh tried to keep the edge of bitterness out of his voice. Accidents happened to people, he'd told himself countless times. There was no sense brooding that his particular disaster had been preventable. He was lucky to be alive and back on his feet.

He did feel a bit disoriented, though. Money wasn't a problem, thanks to the healthy nest egg he'd socked away, but he had to do something with his life. He'd never wanted to end up like his father, running a dive shop on a Florida tourist dock until it was time to retire, then spending every day fishing until it was time to die.

The trouble was, no other future seemed feasible. He had been exactly what he'd always wanted to be—a deep-sea diver. Then the oil company's almost criminal disregard for basic safety on its rigs had ended that career.

Now that he'd been given a medical all-clear for everything but his chosen profession, Josh knew he was going to have to face dreary reality soon. But first, he thought, he would stall a while and see a bit of Scotland, perhaps even the rest of Britain and Europe.

As if reading his mind, Maggie gave his arm a reassuring little pat. "You'll see, Josh," she said cheerfully. "Things will work out. I'm glad you're comin' to the house for dinner tonight. We'll celebrate your clean bill of health." She fussed for a moment with her black, shoulder-length hair, fluffing the strands to dry them, then reached down to the floor for her purse. "What's this?" she asked with a smile as she held up a pair of muddy sandals. "These slippers don't look like your size, Prince Charming. Who's the Cinderella?"

Josh glanced at the shoes and scowled, realizing that Heather had overlooked her sandals when he'd lifted her out of the car and that they'd slipped under the seat so he hadn't noticed them. "A girl I picked up yesterday," he answered absently.

"Picked up?" Maggie echoed, her dark eyes brimming with curiosity and amusement. "So the real Josh Campbell is beginnin' to emerge, is he?"

Remembering all too vividly his body's responses to Heather Sinclair, Josh heaved a sigh. "Part of the real Josh Campbell seems to be coming alive," he admitted with a grin. "But the old self-defense mechanisms need working on. This girl is . . .

well, a *girl*. I mean, she's a woman, but she's not
. . . I couldn't just . . . She's too . . . " He frowned,
wondering why he was sounding so addled, just
as he'd wondered for most of the previous night
and a good part of the day why he hadn't been
able to get Heather out of his mind.

Maggie laughed. "The young lady brought out
more honorable instincts than the usual ones,
and you don't know how to deal with them, is
that it?"

"Exactly!" Josh blurted, then immediately felt
ridiculous. He gave Maggie a sheepish grin. "How
do you manage to pry these confessions out of
me? And how do you know so much in the first
place? You're supposed to be my physiotherapist,
not my psychoanalyst."

"Second sight runs in my family," Maggie in-
formed him breezily.

Josh groaned. "Second sight? As in foretelling
the future? Predicting the vagaries of Fate? Oth-
erworldly stuff? Heather would love you, Maggie."

"Heather, is it? Pretty name. Tell me all about
her."

To Josh's surprise, he did tell Maggie everything he knew about Heather. "But she's not for
me," he said as he pulled into the driveway at the
Tudor cottage where Maggie and her husband
lived. "I don't plan to see Heather again."

"Then how will you return her sandals?" Maggie
asked. "Will you mail them, mud splashes and
all?"

Josh frowned. "I'll clean them up and drop them
off at the reception desk at her office."

Getting out of the car, Maggie picked up Heather's sandals. "We might as well take them in and
clean them up now. And I'll enlist Donald to talk
sense to you about deliverin' them to the girl per-

sonally. Droppin' them off at her office indeed, Josh Campbell. I never thought you'd take the craven coward's way out." Maggie closed the car door with a great flourish, as if to punctuate her last remark.

As Josh followed her, he shook his head and laughed. Maggie Alexander's bullying had pulled him through some bad times, and her husband's calm, compassionate friendship had contributed to the healing process almost as much.

If the two of them wanted to start nagging him about his personal life, Josh thought, he didn't mind. They'd earned the right.

Three hours later, Josh waved good night to the Alexanders, carrying Heather's clean sandals hooked over two fingers. He still planned to drop off the shoes at the *Dreamweavers* office; the kidding he'd endured from both Donald and Maggie hadn't changed his mind about staying away from a woman as vulnerable and trusting as Heather Sinclair.

Just as he reached his car, Josh saw the next-door neighbor's dog bearing down on him. The frisky mongrel named MacBeth still seemed to think of itself as a cute little ball of fluff, but already looked like a small, clumsy horse. "Hey, how ya doin'?" Josh said, grinning and bracing himself for the animal to bound toward him as usual and leap up to plant its great paws on his shoulders, as if eagerly asking for the next waltz.

But the dog spied Heather's shoes, skidded to a stop, and decided on a different amusement. With a sloppy grin, MacBeth caught one sandal between his teeth, growled excitedly, and launched into an enthusiastic game of tug-of-war.

"MacBeth! Cut it out!" Josh said, trying in vain to twist the shoe free. "Lay off, MacBeth!"

The match went on until Josh disgustedly surrendered the shoe, belatedly realizing that the more he fought, the worse shape the sandal was going to be in.

MacBeth stared at him for several moments, then feinted a few teasing moves in an effort to entice Josh back into the fray. Finally catching on that the fun was over, MacBeth gave the shoe a few extra chews for good measure, then dropped it, shooting Josh a look of grave disappointment before wandering off to find a more worthy adversary.

Gingerly picking up the sandal by one soggy strap, Josh examined the damage. "Thanks a lot, MacBeth," he grumbled.

Yet there was a strange lift to his spirits as he realized that Fate had intervened once more. Now he was going to have to see Heather after all.

Five

It took Josh the better part of the next day to find exactly the same sandals as Heather's, and when he showed up at the *Dreamweavers* office, it was almost closing time.

"Is Miss Sinclair here?" he asked.

The woman sitting guard outside the door that he assumed was Heather's looked like somebody's granny as she peered up at Josh through her round, gold-rimmed glasses, patting her head to find one of the several pencils woven into her cloud of blue-white curls. A sign on her desk proclaimed in gold lettering that her name was Mrs. Cameron.

"Whom shall I say wishes to see Miss Sinclair?" Mrs. Cameron asked with the rough but melodic phrasing Josh recognized as Glaswegian. He'd been friends with several men from Glasgow when he'd worked on the oil rig; the accent was unmistakable.

"You can tell Heather that Josh Campbell's here," he answered.

The woman gave him a baleful stare for several moments. "Josh *Campbell*, is it?"

He remembered that Heather had mentioned how the Cameron clan, like so many others, regarded Campbells as little better than Englishmen.

But Heather had been joking when she'd teased him about his name; Josh wasn't sure about Mrs. Cameron. However, if the Scots wanted to carry on their ancient feuds, that was their problem. He wasn't going to apologize to anyone. "Yes, Ma'am," he said firmly. "Josh Campbell."

Mrs. Cameron sniffed, then used the eraser end of the pencil she'd pulled from her hair and punched out a number on her phone. "A Mister . . . " She cleared her throat and gave Josh a look that told him his name was stuck somewhere in her voice box, then tried again. "A Mr. *Campbell* to see you, Miss Sinclair," she intoned, as though she were announcing the arrival of the Four Horsemen.

A moment later, the door to the inner office opened.

Josh gaped at the polished lady who stood in the doorway. "Heather?" he murmured disbelievingly. Her curls were as wayward as ever, but loosely drawn up into a stylish topknot with tendrils framing the even, strong features that were enhanced by artful makeup, the freckles hardly visible. Dressed in flattering shades of gold, from a soft bronze silk-embroidered cashmere bolero over a silk shell and pleated pants of a paler shade of the same color, to the sunny scarf she'd threaded through the waistband loops and fastened in a casual knot at the front with a gold clip, to her tawny Italian leather pumps, Heather projected the kind of throwaway chic Josh admired most.

He realized that if he'd seen this version of Heather Sinclair to start with, he'd have felt perfectly comfortable about being attracted to her.

"Hi," he said quietly, then remembered why he'd come and held up the plastic bag he was carrying. "I have something of yours."

Heather's glance quickly took in the beige slacks, open-necked ivory shirt, and taupe leather wind-breaker that emphasized Josh's rugged goods looks and overwhelming masculinity. Her pulse took off like a racehorse bolting out of the gate. And the disturbing, elusive worries left by a dream she'd had about him but couldn't quite remember sud-denly seemed silly. "Please come in," she said with a tiny smile, standing to one side and indicating her inner office with a vague hand gesture.

When he brushed past her, his nearness set off a startling tremor within Heather's body, his clean, spicy fragrance once again teasing her senses. Certain she would never breathe that scent again without thinking of Josh, she barely managed to give the receptionist a calm smile. "I guess I'll say good night to you now, Jessie," she said, amazed that her voice sounded fairly normal. "It's past time for you to be leaving, and there's no great hurry for those letters you're working on."

Jessie peered over the rim of her glasses into Heather's office. "I could stay a while," she said loudly, to be sure Josh could hear.

"It won't be necessary," Heather said, then winked at the older lady and stepped out into the reception area, half-closing the door behind her. "He's one of the good Campbells, Jess."

"One of the good Campbells?" Jessie asked, add-ing a derisive harrumph. "If there's any such crea-ture. I always remember what my great-grandmother used to say—"

"I know this Campbell," Heather whispered, amused but embarrassed by Jessie's quirk. "Josh is a perfect gentleman, I promise." Unable to resist, she gave Jessie her naughtiest grin and did a creditable Mae West drawl: "He's as pure as the driven snow, if you get my drift."

After staring at Heather for a moment, Jessie chuckled, waving her hand in front of her face as if slapping at a gnat. "The things you say, Heather Sinclair. I swear, if I were your mother, I'd put you right over my knee."

Heather laughed. "No you wouldn't, Jess. You'd spoil me just like Mum does. Now get home to that cute little granddaughter of yours and give her a kiss for me, okay?"

Though Jessie shook her head dubiously, she quickly straightened her desk and picked up her purse. "I'm leavin', but it's against me better judgment, Heather Sinclair. You girls today are too cheeky," the woman muttered on her way to the door. As she put her hand on the knob, she gave Heather a fierce look. "What you need, young lady, is a good strong husband who can control you where others can't."

"If there's any such creature," Heather said in a playful imitation of Jessie's earlier words. What she didn't bother adding was that the kind of husband Jessie had described was exactly the sort of man Heather Sinclair was determined to avoid. She was no sack of oats to be tossed over a broad male shoulder.

Josh was glancing around Heather's spacious office, impressed by the quiet elegance of the antique mahogany furnishings. "That woman carries this Campbell thing a bit far, don't you think?" he asked with a wry smile.

Heather laughed quietly. "Jessie remembers the old clan tales her great-aunts had heard from *their* great-aunts. Don't take her attitude personally. Besides, if you had any reason to want to win

Jessie over, you could do it without a bit of trouble." She paused and glanced at the bag Josh was carrying. "And speaking of trouble, there seems to be no end to what I cause you. I'm sorry about the shoes. I realized yesterday morning that I'd left them in your car, but of course I had no idea how to get in touch with you."

Musing that the effort to replace Heather's sandals was only a minuscule part of the trouble she had given him since he'd met her, Josh merely smiled and handed her the plastic bag. "How are the feet?" he asked.

"I'm as good as new, thanks to your fine doctorin'," Heather said with her put-on Scottish lilt. She was about to set the bag aside when she realized that the shoes were in a box. Wondering why, she took it out and opened it. "These aren't my sandals," she said with a puzzled frown. "They're exactly like mine, but they're new."

"I'm afraid yours met an untimely end," Josh explained. "There's this dog, you see . . . " Quickly, and with some embarrassment, he told Heather about MacBeth's overly enthusiastic friendliness.

"You didn't have to go to all that effort to replace those old sandals," Heather protested, going to her desk to get out her handbag.

"It was no big deal," Josh said with a shrug, watching Heather's every move, still bowled over by how different she seemed from the girl he'd first met. Oddly enough, he couldn't decide which Heather appealed to him more. He liked both of them. But this one seemed more his type—not such a vulnerable young thing. "It was my fault the shoe got wrecked," he added absently, realizing he should leave now that he'd finished his errand, but reluctant to go.

"It was a very big deal for you to replace those

sandals," Heather said as she opened her wallet and took out several bills. "I know, because I've been trying to get a pair just like the old ones and couldn't find them. I'll bet you spent hours searching," Returning to Josh, she thrust out the money.

He looked at it as if it were something slightly distasteful. "If you're trying to pay me for the shoes, forget it."

Heather wasn't at all surprised by his reaction. "Then you have to let me find some other way to thank you for all your kindnesses."

Josh smiled. "How about dinner?" he suggested.

Heather nodded. "Perfect." She gathered up her keys and purse. "I'd love to take you to dinner, though I do have to stop off— "

"No, Heather," Josh interrupted, reaching out to grasp her shoulders, sorely tempted to find out whether the kiss that had been haunting him for two nights had been as soul-searing as he recalled. "I meant that you'd let me take you to dinner."

Gazing at Josh, wishing he would kiss her instead of just looking as if he were considering the idea, Heather gave a shaky laugh. "I'm supposed to thank you by letting you buy me a meal? How generous of me."

"But it's the only thanks I'll accept," Josh said quietly. "Unless you count this. . . ." He grazed his mouth over Heather's soft lips, utterly incapable of resisting the lure of their sweetness. Just as before, he found he couldn't pull back, couldn't resist her velvety mouth, her parted lips, the honeyed taste of her. Before he could stop himself, he was crushing her slender body against his, heady with triumph when her arms crept around his neck and she responded to him with all the eagerness he'd remembered from that first encounter.

Heather experienced a strange urgency, a need only Josh had ever aroused, her soft curves instinctively fitting themselves to his hard, unyielding body, her mouth inviting and welcoming the bold invasion of his tongue. Sapped of all her strength, she clung to Josh in a kind of surrender she hadn't believed possible. Not for her. And surely not a second time!

Suddenly realizing what was happening, she stiffened, placed her palms against Josh's chest, and pushed herself back a little, staring up at him in horror. "I don't understand," she blurted. "This isn't like me, Josh. I've never . . . The way I kiss you, the way you make me feel . . . It's not the way I mean to act."

Josh tried to gather his self-control, knowing exactly how Heather felt. He hadn't meant to kiss her at all, much less devour her the way he had.

Keeping his arms around her, he took several deep breaths, then managed a smile. "What don't you understand, Muffin? The situation seems pretty clear to me."

"Maybe to you, but to me it's very confusing." Trembling, she was grateful for the steadying strength of Josh's arms, the bulwark of his body. But she scowled even at that reaction. Why was it that a single kiss from Josh, even a look, a touch, or merely the sound of his voice, could so thoroughly weaken her sense of independence, her almost desperate conviction that she had to resist her compelling attraction to him?

Josh reached up to trace the creases in her forehead with the tip of his index finger. "Didn't your mother ever tell you your face would freeze that way?" he said, his whole being awash with the now-familiar tenderness Heather aroused in him.

Heather gently extricated herself from his arms and moved back to her desk to get her handbag and keys. She'd had enough of acting like a love-struck fool. "I absolutely insist that dinner is my treat," she said as she walked briskly past Josh to open the office door, determined to assert herself. If she bought him a meal as thanks for his efforts to replace her sandals, she might stop feeling the undermining force of his protectiveness. Perhaps she could turn him into a friend. A buddy. The way she did with most men. It was a neat trick all the Sinclair women had learned early in life, when their constant travels had taught them that get-ting too involved with anyone meant wrenching sadness at the inevitable departure. "So," she said primly, "are we agreed? Dinner's on me?"

"You sure do like to argue, Heather," Josh said with a grin. "Let's go grab a bite and then discuss the bill."

Moments later they were getting into the small, old-fashioned, gilt-cage elevator he'd come up on earlier. In the close quarters of the tiny lift, Josh breathed in the elusive traces of a very good per-fume. As his glance again took in the cashmere, silk, expensive leather and simple but rich gold jewelry that Heather wore, he realized anew that the *Dreamweavers* version of the bedraggled girl he'd picked up in the rain was his type after all.

Heather was acutely aware of Josh's close scru-tiny. His nearness was playing havoc with her senses, and she was still on fire from the effects of his kiss. For all her concern that his impact on her was too overwhelming, she found herself cra-zily hoping that the elevator would lurch to a stop, throw her against Josh's inviting chest, and leave her stranded in his strong arms until some-one came to the rescue—preferably after several hours. Or weeks.

As the elevator reached street level, Heather suddenly remembered something rather important. "I'd started to tell you before . . . well, before," she murmured, unable to speak much above a husky whisper, "that I have to go to see my friend Maharg before I do anything else tonight. He lives on the outskirts of the city, so I could meet you later, Josh. Or if you'd rather, we could go for dinner another evening."

Opening the door, Josh frowned. If this Maharg character Heather mentioned so often was a rival for her attention, she certainly was open about the man. "How were you planning to get to his place?" he asked carefully.

"On the bus," Heather answered, grateful to leave the confines of the elevator. Marching purposefully through the high-ceilinged foyer of the Georgian town house that had been converted to offices, she tried to banish from her mind the delicious warmth of Josh's lips, the coaxing demands of his tongue. "I don't have a car. In fact, I don't drive."

Josh battled another surge of desire as he watched Heather stride ahead of him, her trim hips swinging provocatively. "And from what I observed the other day," he said in a strained voice, "you don't do too well with buses. Why don't I take you to wherever this Maharg is?" Josh had posed the question deliberately, wondering if Heather would prefer to keep her meeting private.

Heather stopped in her tracks and turned to stare at Josh, surprised by his offer. She'd given him an easy out and he hadn't taken it. "I hate to impose on you to chauffeur me again," she said quietly.

Josh smiled, finding himself hoping she was going to accept. "It's no imposition."

Heather returned his smile. "To be honest, I really would love a ride. I have to change buses twice to get to Maharg's place. And you know, you might enjoy meeting him. He's an interesting person."

As Josh cupped his hand under Heather's elbow to leave the building and guide her to his car, he realized that her answer had mattered far too much to him; he'd never wanted to be that dependent on the whims of a woman. Yet he couldn't help being relieved that she seemed unconcerned about his meeting her friend.

It crossed Josh's mind that Heather might be playing one man against the other; the occasional lady had tried that game with him before. But he quickly brushed the idea aside, certain that Heather wouldn't do that sort of thing. "What kind of name is Maharg?" he asked.

"It's Graham spelled backward," Heather said, breathing deeply, beginning to relax a bit as a warm breeze soothed her frayed nerves. She turned to smile up at Josh and was beguiled all over again by the way he looked, the late afternoon sun painting strands of gold in his fair hair and turning his hazel eyes to warm amber. "Maharg's real name is Sir Alasdair Graham," she explained a bit breathlessly. "He claims his family was outlawed several generations ago and couldn't use it's own surname, so some of its members simply reversed the letters. Eventually they were returned to their rightful positions—the family *and* the letters—but Sir Alasdair is just enough of an old curmudgeon to enjoy using the name of the former outcasts."

Josh smiled, inordinately pleased by Heather's description of Maharg. The man didn't sound much like a rival. "What could a woman like you have in common with an old curmudgeon?" he asked as they reached his car.

"Maharg is hosting a clan gathering in a few weeks. It's to be the kickoff weekend of a *Dream-weavers* train tour of Scotland for a rather large contingent of Americans who are his distant cousins on his late mother's side," Heather explained, then grinned at Josh. "They're MacDonalds."

Opening the car door for Heather, Josh groaned. "So by driving you to this man's place, I'm letting myself in for another session of Campbell-bashing?"

Laughing, Heather shook her head. "I don't think so. Maharg doesn't take old feuds as seriously as Jessie Cameron does. But be prepared. He can seem cranky." She gave Josh a meaningful look, remembering how he'd scolded her when he'd tended the wounds on her feet. "Like some other gentleman of my acquaintance, who shall remain nameless for the moment."

"Has it ever occurred to you, Heather Sinclair, that there are times when you just might bring out the Billy Goat Gruff in a man?"

Heather merely laughed again. "Wrong, Josh Campbell. Maharg is the soul of patience with me. You just watch."

Josh whistled softly as he drove up the long, broad, tree-lined drive toward a stone house that looked like a structural history of Scotland, all the disparate parts thrown together as if by a mad architect: Turrets and arrow-slits in the section that was a medieval castle; the classical lines of the Renaissance; an imitation Brighton Pavilion of the Regency period; the gingerbread gazebo of the Victorian era. A television antenna represented the twentieth century. "And I thought MacBeth was a mongrel," Josh said with a low whistle. "This place defies definition."

"And it has its share of ghosts and bloodcurdling history," Heather said delightedly as she and Josh got out of the car. "Maharg told me about a possessive, ambitious, fabulously beautiful but vengeful mistress of one of his ancestors. A woman scorned, she stabbed the laird to death just because he refused to marry her, and then did herself in as well. Now she patrols the corridors of the castle section, determined to drive intruders out of what she coveted in life as her rightful and private property. I'm on the verge of persuading Maharg to let me include his house on a regular tour of Scotland's haunted mansions; the clan gathering is the test case. If it goes well, Maharg and I will make a deal. I know he could use the money, and my clients would love this place."

"He needs money?" Josh asked, surprised. "I know the taxes on these properties can be backbreaking, but doesn't Maharg have a family to help him?"

Heather shook her head. "He's a bachelor. Very alone in the world except for a few cronies, his housekeeper, and his servants." She smiled as a tall, distinguished man with a neatly clipped white mustache and angular but ruddy cheeks came around from the rear of the house. "There's Maharg now," she said quietly to Josh. "Isn't he perfect?"

Josh smiled. Sir Alasdair Graham, a gentleman of indeterminate years, was the epitome of the laird of the Scottish manor from bygone days with his Harris tweeds, gray porkpie hat perched over his white hair at a jaunty angle, and a carved walking stick that he began waving as soon as he spied Heather. "It's about time you got here, young lady!" he grumbled, stomping along the driveway toward her, his body so erect it was obvious it needed the stick only for effect.

"The soul of patience, huh?" Josh murmured.

"That's just his way," Heather said with a grin, then went to plant a kiss on the older man's weathered cheek. "So what's the crisis today?" she asked cheerfully.

"It's that blasted driver I've hired," Maharg growled, his stern features rather forbidding. "He doesn't know a blasted thing about cars, blasted young fool."

Josh suppressed a smile. He had the feeling that the word "blasted," Maharg's concession to the presence of a lady, represented a lot of other more colorful epithets.

Heather laughed. "You mean you didn't ask me to come out to solve a problem with the party?"

"What problem?" Maharg snapped, scowling at her. "There's no problem, though Mrs. Dalrymple is after me to go over the menus, and it's my opinion she should talk to you about such things. What do I know about menus? Then the blasted car went on the blasted blink, so that was another reason to get you out here."

"But I don't know the first thing about cars," Heather protested good-naturedly.

"You're an American, aren't you?" Maharg said as if making an accusation.

"Well, yes, but—"

"I thought all Americans knew about cars."

Heather looked back at Josh and winked at him. She wanted to introduce the two men, but first she had to tease Maharg a bit. "Right. All Americans know about cars," she said with a grin. "Just like all you Brits play cricket."

"Don't call me a Brit!" Maharg said vehemently,

his eyes flashing blue fire. "I'm a Scot! And I wouldn't waste my time on the likes of cricket. Shinty's my game, or was when I was a young man. Speaking of young men, who's this you've brought with you?"

"This is Josh Campbell," Heather said. "He was kind enough to give me a ride."

Maharg looked Josh up and down as the two men exchanged a handshake. "I'd like to see this one on my shinty team," Maharg said with an approving nod.

"What's shinty?" Heather asked, musing that Josh Campbell would be a welcome addition to any kind of team. To any kind of activity. Especially . . . She stopped herself before her wayward thoughts could wander too far into forbidden territory.

"Shinty's a man's game," Maharg said by way of explanation. "A drinking man's game."

"It's a form of field hockey, isn't it, sir?" Josh asked politely. "Originally played with clubs and a wooden ball? I'm told it might have been the forerunner of ice hockey."

Maharg chuckled. "Ice hockey is for pantywaists. Shinty's a thousand times more interesting. Turns into a rousing brawl if the players have any real spirit—or enough good malt spirits. You're an American, Campbell. Do you know anything about cars?"

Josh nodded. "I used to tinker with them when I was a kid. And I've worked in a couple of garages."

"Come with me," Maharg said tersely. He started off toward a group of buildings to the left of the driveway.

Josh turned to glance at Heather. When she shrugged and grinned, they both set off to trail along behind Maharg.

Heather was amazed by Maharg's instant acceptance of Josh. The Scot rarely took to outsiders. But she hadn't meant to get Josh involved in trying to give automotive advice. "If you have car troubles, why don't you take it to a repairman?" she asked Maharg when they reached the low buildings that had been converted from stables to garages some years before.

Maharg glowered at her. "Those places are full of more of those blasted young fools who don't know anything. And they want to tow the car in to have a look at it. Tow it! As if I would allow such a thing. Everybody's like doctors nowadays —no house calls. The world's gone mad."

Josh stopped in his tracks, gaping at the gleaming black car that was revealed when Maharg unlocked the door of the end cubicle. "Good lord, sir, that's a 1955 Bentley," Josh said. "And it looks as if it just rolled out of the factory. It's fantastic."

"You know your cars, Campbell," Maharg said, obviously pleased and impressed.

"How do you know the year?" Heather asked Josh, even more impressed than Maharg was. Knowing almost nothing about cars herself, she was amazed that someone could recognize a certain model at a glance.

Josh smiled at her. "Some guys play with electric trains," he said with a self-deprecating laugh. "Others of us get hooked on vintage automobiles."

Maharg's mind was back on the immediate problem. "Can't figure out what's wrong," he muttered. "This lady ran like a top until yesterday. She was the last one too."

"Last one?" Josh asked, his excitement growing. For a classic-car buff to stumble onto even one treasure such as the Bentley was like a prospector falling into an undiscovered gold mine. The possibility that there were other nuggets behind the line of closed doors was mind-boggling. "What do you mean, the last one?" Josh asked carefully.

"The last of my cars," Maharg said. "Since my chauffeur retired five years ago and went to live with his son in Australia, the vehicles have decided one by one that they should retire too. These old dears need constant care, but do you think I can find someone who knows the first thing about fixing them? I've a mind to send that new chap packing. He's a good driver, and I suppose he means well enough, but what's the use of a car that won't start and a driver who can't figure out what the trouble is?"

Josh surveyed the doors, wishing he had the temerity to ask to see what lay behind them.

Noticing the direction of Josh's glance and the excitement in his eyes, Heather couldn't resist acting on sudden impulse. "I've never seen your fleet of cars, Maharg," she said with a grin. "Could we have a look at them?"

"Don't know why you'd want to," Maharg grumbled. "But go ahead."

Josh decided that if he weren't already enchanted with Heather Sinclair, her inspired "open sesame" would have cast the fatal spell.

"Campbell, if you think you can do something for any of these blasted engines, tinker to your heart's content. I'm going back to the house to tell Mrs. Dalrymple to get a tea tray ready."

"Oh, there's no need, Maharg," Heather protested, not sure how Josh would feel about sticking around for tea. "We're on our way . . . " Her voice trailed off as she saw the shadow of disappointment in Maharg's eyes.

Noticing the same thing, Josh put his hand on Heather's waist and squeezed lightly, surprising himself with the naturalness of the gesture. "I'd like some tea," he said quietly but firmly.

Grateful for Josh's sensitivity, and electrified by the warm strength of his large hand on her waist, Heather managed only a shaky smile and a soft, "I would too."

Maharg looked from Heather to Josh and back again, nodded, and started away, only to stop after he'd taken three steps. "Come to the garden behind the house after you've had a look around here. You'll need this, Campbell," he said, tossing Josh a key ring. "For the garage doors."

Josh made an easy catch with his free hand, not releasing Heather even after Maharg had walked away.

Heather told herself to go with Maharg. Something in the pressure of Josh's hand told her that he wasn't running from her the way he had been two days before, the way he should still be running. But it was as if he were a magnet and she were endowed with about as much self-determination as an iron filing. She couldn't move.

She held her breath, waiting—for what, she wasn't sure.

Six

Josh smiled down at Heather as he felt the guardedness that seemed to vibrate through her body. "Thanks," he murmured, increasing the pressure to draw her closer and turn her to face him, clasping his hands at the back of her waist. "When it comes to classic cars, I'm like a kid, I guess. It was thoughtful of you to notice that I wanted to peek behind those doors."

Though Josh's grin was endearingly boyish, Heather couldn't think of him as anything but a startingly virile, full-grown man, whose every touch made her more aware of her vulnerability. "Do you think you actually might be able to do something for Maharg?" she asked, her eyes fixed on Josh's strong chin; she couldn't meet his gaze.

"I imagine so," he said confidently. "Fixing up old cars has been my main passion for years." It occurred to him that another passion was beginning to capture an unexpectedly firm foothold in him. It was a disturbing prospect. Adept at guarding his independence, he wasn't sure he was ready to give up even a shred of it. Yet he felt it slipping away from him. "Apart from diving, that is," he added as a vague afterthought.

"Diving?" Heather repeated. "Is that what you did in the oil industry? Were you working on the North Sea rigs as a deep-sea diver?"

Josh realized that he'd inadvertently opened up a subject he didn't feel like discussing. "Yeah," he answered after a moment.

A vivid memory skimmed through Heather's mind, a scene she'd watched with horror on a television newscast. *Ten months*, she thought, the time factor clicking into place. Josh had said he'd been in Edinburgh for about ten months. She clearly recalled having come back from a trip to the States ten months before, just in time to watch nightly telecasts showing a disastrous explosion on a North Sea oil rig. No one had been killed, but there had been serious injuries.

Even at the time, she remembered, she'd been particularly haunted by that catastrophe. With all the dreadful events that filled television screens nearly every evening at news time, the oil-rig explosion had been the one that had shaken her.

Suddenly, for a fleeting but awful instant, she saw Josh thrown across the rig's platform by the force of an explosion, hit by flying debris, and landing like a rag doll, his body shattered. An almost physical pain gripped her; she wanted to fly back through time to drag him away from danger, to spare him, to comfort him.

Staring at Heather as he felt a convulsive shudder pass through her body, Josh was certain that somehow she knew exactly what had happened to him. "What's wrong?" he asked gently, shocked by the fear in her eyes.

Heather said nothing, trying to collect her wits. She looked at Josh as if to check that he really was all right. "I . . . I think I should go up to the house and talk to Mrs. Dalrymple," she murmured. If the horrible vision she'd just experienced, along with the undercurrent of anxiety she hadn't been able to shake completely since meeting Josh, meant she actually was gifted in a small way with some kind of second sight, she wasn't overly thrilled to discover her psychic powers. These strange moments weren't part of the harmless metaphysical nonsense she half-pretended to dabble in. They weren't fun. They were terrifying. "This clan gathering of Maharg's is important to *Dreamweavers*, as well as to him," she added hastily, wanting to talk of normal things, things that made sense.

"Heather, are you all right?" Josh asked, crooking his index finger under her chin to make her look up at him.

"I'm fine," she said with a forced smile.

She'd answered too quickly, Josh thought. "No you're not, Muffin. You're upset. And it has something to do with me. With what happened to me."

Heather gazed at him for a long moment, then slumped against him, sliding her arms around his waist. "You were hurt," she whispered. "You almost died. And it was so unnecessary. Another company skimping on safety measures."

Josh stiffened, at the same time wrapping his arms tightly around her. "How do you know?"

She tilted back her head and looked up at him. "I'm not sure. Just now I felt as if I could see the explosion as clearly as if I were there. But there's probably a rational explanation. After all, I did watch the television reports when it happened, and the timing matches with what you told me about coming to Edinburgh ten months ago, so probably all the separate facts just started to fit together to form a picture in my mind . . . "

"What's this?" Josh said, his voice hoarse with emotion. He had to tease Heather or be caught up in feelings that were too strong and too uncanny to face. "Is Heather Sinclair, of all people, trying to explain away the mysteries of the universe with logic?"

Heather laughed. "Hey, that's right," she said, managing not to sound too shaky. "If I'm not careful, I'll damage my fey reputation."

"Oh, I wouldn't worry too much about that," Josh said with deliberate ambiguity.

They stood for several moments, just holding each other, both of them trying to sort out what was happening.

Heather tipped back her head and looked up at Josh. "Are you going to fight back?" she asked. "The oil company, I mean? They shouldn't get away with what happened."

Josh shrugged. "I've fired off a few letters; all I get is some public-affairs hack writing some supposedly soothing garbage about impending investigations. What's the point in trying to battle the giants? You can't beat 'em."

"If you fight, you stand a good chance of getting nowhere," Heather admitted. "But if you don't fight, you stand an even better chance of it. You can't just—" She stopped, realizing that she had no business telling Josh what he should or shouldn't do. He probably wanted to put the whole horrible disaster out of his mind. And who could blame him if he did? "I really must go up to the house and talk to Mrs. Dalrymple about those menus," she said hastily. "I think I know what the problem is," she added with a quiet laugh as she moved out of Josh's arms. "Maharg wants to serve haggis to his American guests, and Mrs. Dalrymple refuses. I'm with her; authenticity has no place in fantasy, and a dish that consists of organ meats boiled in a sheep's stomach is a little too authentic for my taste."

Josh was surprised to discover how much he was beginning to like Heather Sinclair. He even appreciated her remarks about battling the profit-mongers whose negligence had cost him and a lot of other workers so much pain. She was wrong, of course; he was no David to take on a multinational Goliath. But there was something shining and sweet about her naive idealism. "I've tasted haggis, so you and Mrs. Dalrymple get my vote," he said absently as he watched Heather walk back up the driveway toward the house, her trim hips swaying with each stride of her long legs.

Heather looked back at him, grinning. "Thanks. I'll count on you, because I have a feeling that if you can fix Maharg's cars, your vote will count for more than Mrs. Dalrymple's and mine put together."

As he followed the path at the side of Maharg's house toward the rear, where he assumed he would find the garden, Josh was lost in thought, bemused not only by the collection of almost mint-condition cars he'd found behind the garage doors, but by everything that had happened since he'd met Heather.

He couldn't stop thinking about her strange vision of the explosion, about the sense of connection he felt with her, about the way she made him want to live up to a better image of himself.

The woman even had him thinking that perhaps he should battle after all for the chance to have his say at some of the so-called impending investigations into the oil-rig mishap that had come close to taking his life. By backing down so quickly from telling him he should fight, Heather had gotten to him where it hurt—his pride. And his unresolved anger.

Glancing toward the hazy purple mountains in the distance, Josh smiled, wondering whether it really was magic that was affecting him like a mind-altering drug.

Probably just thin air, he told himself.

He moved quietly along the path's worn-down grass, noting the Gothic-arched windows and low, heavy doorways of the house. He could see why Heather wanted to include the eccentric old mansion on her ghost-hunting tours. He wouldn't have been the least bit surprised to see a shrouded phantom or a headless specter wandering toward him.

Suddenly, from one of the open windows just ahead—a kitchen window, if the pie cooling on the sill was a clue—he caught the distinctive, light cadence of women talking and laughing together, a sound he hadn't heard in just that way for more than two decades. Its impact caught him hard in the solar plexus, dealing out the kind of emotional sucker punch no one could be braced for. He stopped dead, thrust back in his imagination to a time of innocence when he'd taken for granted something as simple and reassuring as women's voices in a kitchen.

Clenching his hands into tight fists, Josh took several deep breaths as a flood of memory washed over him. He was experiencing another of the confrontations with his past that had been recurring with disturbing frequency since his long convalescence had robbed him of his usual escape hatches of hard work and harder play—and since Maggie Alexander and some unbelievably dedicated, compassionate nurses had shaken his cynical beliefs about womankind in general.

Though he didn't listen deliberately to the conversation between Heather and Maharg's housekeeper, he found himself edging closer to the window, becoming aware of an unfamiliar lilting voice that sounded like a gentler, friendlier version of Heather's receptionist.

"Och, Heather," the woman was saying with a roll of the last syllable that turned the name into the whisper of a breeze through tiny petals, "there's not thanks enough for all the help you've been."

"I'm just doing my job," Josh heard Heather protest. "Besides, helping to organize a clan gathering is a wonderful experience. I've loved every minute."

"You've not fooled me, lass," Mrs. Dalrymple said. "I know you've gone far past the call of duty, not to mention that you've made sure there'd be a healthy profit for Sir Alasdair instead of another drain on his purse."

"That's part of my job as well," Heather answered. "You can be sure the hotels and restaurants and all the other facilities we use do very well for themselves. And nobody who's comin' here on our tour expects a free ride at Maharg Place. Indeed, why should they?"

Josh smiled as he noticed that Heather's voice had taken on a lilt very much like the housekeeper's. He was certain her mimicry was totally unconscious, and unsurprising, considering that Mrs. Dalrymple's Glasgow burr was exactly like Jessie Cameron's. Heather was just impressionable enough to pick up the speech habits she heard so often.

Deciding he should make his presence known rather than just slip past the window, he knocked gently on the door nearest the open window. "Mrs. Dalrymple?" he asked with a tentative smile when the trim woman opened the door. He laughed inwardly at himself for having half-expected a portly Queen Victoria type in a gray dress and a starched white apron. The real Mrs. Dalrymple wore a green linen dress and a floral scarf knotted rather rakishly at the neckline; her white hair was short but not severe, her makeup light and subtly flattering. Josh immediately liked her. "I'm Josh Campbell," he said with a friendly smile. "I'm with Heather." Odd, he thought, how he liked saying those words.

"Pleased to meet you, Mr. Campbell," the woman said, offering him her hand, then showing him into the kitchen. "Heather tells me my sister gave you a wee bit of a hard time earlier today."

Josh scowled in puzzlement. "Your sister?"

"Jessie Cameron," Heather explained as she rose from the large wooden table where she'd been sitting in the large, old-fashioned kitchen. She had to move around if only to get rid of some of the nervous energy Josh's arrival had caused; her heart was skipping and racing with the abandon of a child in an unsupervised playground. Josh's large frame and deep voice seemed to dominate the room, his electrifying presence charging the air, altering the very atmosphere. "My receptionist is Mrs. Dalrymple's sister," Heather added, pitching in to help the housekeeper prepare trays of snacks. "Jessie recommended *Dreamweavers* to Maharg for the clan gathering, which landed us the entire tour."

Josh nodded, his smile fading as he braced

DON'T HOLD BACK!

1. **No obligation!** No purchase necessary! Enter our Sweepstakes for a chance to win!
2. **FREE!** Get your first shipment of 6 Loveswept books *and* a lighted makeup case as a free gift.
3. **Save money!** Become a member and every month you get 6 books for the price of 5! Return any shipment you don't want.
4. **Be the first!** You'll always receive your Loveswept books before they are available in stores. You'll be the first to thrill to these exciting new stories.

BANTAM BOOKS' DREAM MAKER SWEEPSTAKES

Entry Form

YES! I want to see where passion will lead me!

Place FREE ENTRY Sticker Here   Place FREE BOOKS Sticker Here

Enter me in the sweepstakes! I have placed my FREE ENTRY sticker on the heart.

Send me six *free* Loveswept novels *and* my *free* lighted makeup case! I have placed my FREE BOOKS sticker on the heart.

Mend a broken heart. Use both stickers to get the most from this special offer!   10355

NAME_____

ADDRESS_____ APT._____

CITY_____

STATE_____ ZIP_____

Loveswept's Heartfelt Promise to You!

There's no purchase necessary to enter the sweepstakes. There is no obligation to buy when you send for your free books and lighted makeup case. You may preview each new shipment for 15 days free. If you decide against it, simply return the shipment within 15 days and owe nothing. If you keep them, pay only $2.09 per book — a savings of 41¢ per book (plus postage, handling, and sales tax in NY and IL.)

Prices subject to change. Orders subject to approval.
See complete sweepstakes rules at the back of this book.   BR234

Detach here and mail today.

Give in to love and see where passion leads you!
Enter the Dream Maker Sweepstakes and send
for your FREE lighted makeup case and 6
FREE Loveswept books today!

(See details inside.)

himself for Mrs. Dalrymple to show the same low regard for Campbells her sister had. "That's terrific," he said lamely.

"You mustn't mind Jess," Mrs. Dalrymple said. "She tends to forget what century she's livin' in. When she was wee, her head was filled with tales of Campbell treachery against the Camerons, who of course were always portrayed as the innocent victims in every quarrel."

Josh was having trouble absorbing everything, especially when the mere act of glancing at Heather seemed to fog up his mind. Searching for something sociable to talk about, he fastened upon something that did make him curious. "Your sister is *Mrs.* Cameron," he pointed out. "Which makes her part of the clan only by marriage, doesn't it?"

Mrs. Dalrymple placed two silver teapots on a tray. "Jess and I were born Camerons," she answered, returning Josh's smile. "I think when Jess married another Cameron—no relation, mind you—she was more interested in the man's name than in the kind of husband he'd be, much to her later regret." The housekeeper glanced pointedly at Heather. "Many's the young lady who makes the same sort of mistake, decidin' ahead of time that she wants this or that triflin' detail in the man of her dreams, and blindin' herself to some good lad who doesn't happen to fit her specifications."

Feeling a crimson flush steal over her cheeks, Heather regretted the times she'd spouted her playful talk about The Right Man to Jessie and her sister over endless cups of tea.

Josh suppressed a grin and wished he had Maggie's second sight, if it involved mind reading. Heather's blush was as intriguing as Mrs. Dalrymple's pointed little lecture. "Could you use a hand to carry things out?" he asked the housekeeper as she picked up one of the trays.

"Well now, isn't that good of you," she said, handing him the tray. "Improper as it may seem to let guests pitch in, I most certainly would appreciate the help. The days are long gone when I had a whole battery of maids to do my biddin', so we don't stand on ceremony around this house. And this bein' Finch's day off, I'm even more shorthanded."

"Finch is the butler," Heather explained as she picked up one of the other trays. "He's been the family retainer for decades. Maybe forever." She lowered her voice to a stage whisper. "I think he's immortal, actually. A benign vampire."

Laughing, Josh winked at Heather as they both fell in line behind Mrs. Dalrymple to follow her out of the kitchen and down a promisingly spooky, narrow passageway to a door at the back of the house, where they stepped outside onto a large stone terrace.

As Josh placed his tray on the terrace's white wrought-iron table, he almost laughed aloud. His former self never would have believed this scene possible: Josh Campbell, helping two ladies serve tea and pretty little sandwiches in a slightly gone-to-seed Scottish garden.

"Here we are, Sir Alasdair," Mrs. Dalrymple said to Maharg, who was glaring reproachfully at an idle marble fountain in the middle of the garden, looking as if he was considering giving the Adonis sculpture a good swift kick in the posterior.

"Now the blasted fountain has fizzled out. Everything around here is going. Next it'll be me,"

Maharg grumbled as he joined the others on the terrace. "Any luck?" he asked, looking at Josh.

"The Bentley's fine," Josh answered. "It was just an exposed wire causing a short. I wrapped it with electrical tape; it'll do until I can get a new wire to put in."

Maharg scowled. "Sounds simple enough. Why didn't the driver know that?"

"Anyone could have missed the problem, sir. It's something I happen to have run into before." Josh smiled pleasantly. "And I have a proposition for you, if you'd care to hear it."

Heather and Mrs. Dalrymple exchanged secret smiles, both of them aware that Josh had endeared himself to Maharg forever, first by fixing the Bentley, then by refusing to puff up his own importance at the expense of the chauffeur.

Heather's whole being was infused with pride, as if she personally had something to do with what a fine man Josh Campbell was. As if he belonged to her.

But during the next few minutes, as Josh offered to spend a few afternoons doing the repairs on Maharg's vehicles and teaching the driver some tricks of the trade, she found herself deeply disturbed again. The more drawn she was to Josh, the more determined she was to resist. She gave herself any number of good reasons, from the simple fact that Josh probably wouldn't be in Scotland much longer to her firm determination not to fall in love with any man for at least another couple of years.

Fall in love, she thought, taken aback.

It couldn't be, Heather told herself. She hardly knew Josh Campbell. How could she fall in love with a man she didn't know?

Besides, he absolutely, beyond any doubt, was not her One And Only.

Unfortunately, as she watched Josh effortlessly win the trust and friendship of her old friend Maharg, and of Mrs. Dalrymple, Heather knew that unless she gathered all possible defenses against his impact, Josh could—if he cared to— steal her heart with ease.

And somehow she was certain it would be a catastrophe if he did.

"Mrs. Dalrymple's little tea party managed to be pretty filling," Josh said as he and Heather drove away from Maharg's estate. "I don't know about you, but I'm not very hungry. Maybe we should take a rain check on dinner." What he really was doing was giving Heather a graceful out. She was edgy with him, clearly unnerved by feelings she didn't want to acknowledge or allow. "How about a drink?" he added, leaving the door open in case he'd misinterpreted Heather's tension.

Heather longed to accept, but she opted for what seemed like better sense. "I think the rain check is a good idea. We stayed at Maharg's longer than I expected to, and I really should go home. Of course, I don't expect you to drive me all the way there," she said hastily. "If you'll just drop me off at a bus stop . . ."

"Don't say it, Heather," Josh said, disappointed that she'd taken the out he'd offered and not at all pleased by her infernal displays of independence or fear or whatever it was that made her talk about taking buses rather than accepting a ride with him. "I'll drive you home, all right? There's no need for you to be so skittish about being alone with me."

"No?" Heather answered, hugging the passenger door as she instinctively made sure there was plenty of space separating her from Josh. "How about the fact that every time you kiss me or even touch me I act like a . . . a love-starved nymphet? Wouldn't you say that's reason enough for anyone to be skittish?"

As usual, Josh was taken aback by Heather's startling bluntness. He'd expected her to protest against his words; he certainly hadn't been prepared for her outright admission of the reason for her behavior. "For some people, those feelings are reason enough to be anything but skittish," he said quietly.

Heather folded her hands tightly in her lap like a prim schoolgirl and said nothing.

They drove in uncomfortable silence for a long while, until finally Josh exploded. "Dammit, do you have to cower as if I'm about to attack you? You make me feel like one of those monsters you claimed to see in my eyes. Believe me, Muffin, you can relax. I'm no big bad wolf who goes after pretty little girls. I'll drop you at your door without so much as a kiss on the cheek, if it'll make you happy."

"What would make me happy would be if you'd kindly stop referring to me as a little girl," Heather said through clenched teeth. "I'm nearly twenty-four, and I'm a very independent, responsible woman. I don't appreciate being patronized. And for the record, I do not cower. Not even from you."

"You're twenty-four?" Josh repeated, clapping his hand to his forehead in mock horror. "No wonder you're driving me up the wall! I haven't gone out with a female that young since I was eighteen."

"You have a habit of robbing the rocking chair, do you?" Heather shot back.

"I have a habit of choosing grown-up women who know better than to tease a man one minute and shrink from him the next."

Heather glared at him, her eyes filling with sudden, infuriating tears. "I wasn't teasing, and I'm not *shrinking* from you. But you know as well as I do that I'd be crazy to let this . . . this ridiculously uncontrollable attraction get out of hand. I'm not experienced enough for you, for one thing. I'm also not up to having an affair with a man I hardly know who could be leaving the country any week or even any day, and I'm—" She stopped, realizing that she'd almost admitted to Josh, and to herself, that she was just plain scared.

"You're what?" he asked, wondering why she'd stopped so suddenly.

Heather searched for something honest to say that wouldn't sound as foolish as the stark truth. "I'm happy with my life as it is. I don't want to complicate it," she said at last, adding what she assumed would be the clincher: "And mere desire would never be enough for me, no matter how powerful it is."

Josh stared at the road, gripping the car's wheel as if he thought it were about to fly off the steering column. "So you're holding out for the whole hearts-and-flowers routine, is that it?"

"Right. The whole thing," Heather answered defiantly.

"Which just goes to show how young and naive you really are," Josh muttered.

Heather lapsed into silence again, and nothing more was said until Josh pulled up in front of her house.

Heather put her hand on the car door's handle.

"Thanks for the ride," she said quietly. "And . . . and for the shoes." She remembered to grab the plastic bag he'd given her earlier. "I wish you'd let me reimburse you."

Josh shook his head. "You promised me a dinner, and that's all I'll accept."

Cocking her head to one side, Heather scowled at him. "You still want to go out to dinner with me?"

Josh leaned both arms on the steering wheel, studying the stars he could see through the windshield, saying nothing for several seconds. Finally he heaved a deep sigh. "Yeah," he answered, wondering even as he heard his monosyllabic reply why he wasn't using his usual good sense and just giving up on this lost cause.

"Why?" Heather asked in a small voice.

He turned to look at her, then laughed. "Beats me," he said. "But give the idea some thought. I'm sure I'll see you out at Maharg's one of these days; maybe by then we both will have cooled down enough to talk things over with a grain of sense on somebody's side."

Heather nodded and managed a tiny smile. "Probably," she said, hoping he was right. "By the way, it was nice of you to offer to help Maharg with the cars."

"My pleasure." Josh shrugged. "I'll enjoy the project. And it gives me another excuse to put off going home."

Heather was surprised by his comment. "Why do you want to put it off? Don't you want to go home?"

Instead of answering, Josh got out of the car and went around to Heather's side. "Don't you?" he asked with a smile. "Want to go home, I mean?"

Realizing that she'd crossed an invisible line

into territory Josh didn't care to discuss with her, Heather lifted her chin and returned his smile, cooling it by several degrees. "The truth is, I probably won't see you before you do head for the States, so as you said to me the other day, good-bye, good luck, it's been interesting knowing you."

Hurrying into her house, aware that Josh was standing by his car watching her, she refused to give in to the inexplicable sadness that threatened to overwhelm her.

Seven

Heather was glad she was wearing an outfit she felt good in when Maharg summoned her to his place to handle yet another crisis in the long count-down to his clan gathering, still three weeks away. Her taupe cotton blazer, white shell, and straight black skirt were businesslike. Stylish but no-nonsense. Power dressing. Just what she needed.

Her hair was loose—much too casual. So she whipped it up into its more sophisticated top-knot, from which only a few tendrils escaped. Her favorite gold, Celtic-design, antique earrings added just the right touch of panache to boost her morale, and after a quick refresher of makeup and perfume, Heather almost felt up to facing the inevitable.

The inevitable meeting with Josh.

There were moments when she regretted having introduced him to Maharg. Every time she went to the estate, Josh was there, supposedly working on the cars but always summoned to the house for the little tea party that had become a ritual.

And as if socializing with him when other people were around wasn't bad enough, Josh always insisted on driving her home afterward.

Heather dreaded those rides with Josh—his infuriatingly relaxed manner, his oh-so-easy conversation, as if he'd forgotten whatever attraction he might have felt for her, as if not a single spark had ever crackled between them. He never seemed to miss an opportunity to demonstrate that he'd decided she really was just a little girl.

Heather brooded for the entire bus journey to Maharg's estate, fantasizing about doing something dramatic to show Josh Campbell that Heather Sinclair was woman enough for the likes of him, whether he thought so or not.

But her better sense prevailed. Vamping just wasn't one of her talents; a rose between her teeth would just look hilarious. Besides, short of jumping into the lap of Maharg's portly driver or throwing herself at the butler, she couldn't think of anything that would wipe the almost-smug smile off Josh's maddeningly handsome face.

She suppressed a giggle as Maharg's cadaverous butler opened the massive main door and peered down his beaked nose at her.

"Hiya, Finch," Heather said with a grin, deliberately teasing him with the casual ways of a generation he claimed to deplore. But she was intrigued by the tall, austere man, as ghostlike an apparition as she'd ever run across. "So what's today's problem?" she asked as the formally attired servant stepped back to show her in.

The hint of a conspiratorial smile passed over his thin lips, but he managed to pull himself together. "I believe Sir Alasdair and Mrs. Dalrymple are at sixes and sevens about the seating arrangements for the Friday night dinner, Miss."

Seating arrangements, Heather thought, exasperated. She'd been summoned all this way and had to go through the tension of facing Josh just to settle a dispute about where people should sit at the dinner table. Her clients, after coming all the way from the States, would be too thrilled at dining in such opulent surroundings to fuss about trifles like that.

In any case, Heather decided, there had to be some other problem to deal with. Even Maharg wouldn't be erratic enough to demand her personal attention for such a minute detail. "Is Mrs. Dalrymple in the kitchen?" she asked.

"No, Miss. Everyone is in the garden at the moment." Finch gave a slight inclination of his head to indicate that Heather should follow him.

Everyone, Heather thought, including Josh, no doubt.

On the way through the house, she noticed small repairs that had been made recently: a broken table leg, a chipped section of the stairway banister, the once-tattered seat and back of a cane chair—all as good as new. "Maharg seems to have hired someone to do a bit of sprucing-up around the place," she remarked.

"Mr. Campbell has been helping out," Finch said in his funereal monotone. He led her toward the terrace through the Grand Ballroom, which was to be used, for the first time in two decades, for the clan gathering, and Heather saw that the cleaning company she'd recommended for temporary household staff had sent a pair of workers who were diligently scrubbing everything in sight.

As she approached the terrace, she saw spouts of water frolicking in the middle of the garden. Her eyebrows shot up in puzzled surprise. "Did

Mr. Campbell fix the fountain too?" she asked jokingly.

"Mr. Campbell seems to have the knack for fixing anything, Miss," Finch answered as he opened one of the French doors that took up most of the outside ballroom wall.

Isn't Mr. Campbell wonderful! Heather thought, stabbed by an inexplicable and totally unreasonable shaft of anger.

"There you are," Maharg said, leaping out of his chair with what struck Heather as renewed vigor. He looked rather dapper, too, she mused, his tweeds well-pressed, his porkpie hat nowhere in sight, his eyes sparkling with inner excitement. "We're having ourselves a tall, cool drink on this balmy day," he said jovially. "What's your pleasure, lass?"

Heather's glance sought out Josh and lingered there, despite her resolve to treat him with the same cavalier indifference he offered her. Mesmerized by the molten gold of his eyes, she felt her resentment of him dissipating, her pulse leaping out of control, her limbs succumbing to a familiar, troubling languor. Had she imagined the flicker of pleasure in his steady gaze? "Hi," she said softly, then guiltily remembered to greet Mrs. Dalrymple as well.

The housekeeper, aglow in a pink linen suit, rose from her chair and went to the wrought-iron table, where there were two frosty pitchers and some highball glasses. "We have gin coolers as well as some lemonade, dear."

"Lemonade would be perfect," Heather said, trying not to notice the sunlight glinting in Josh's hair.

"Have a seat," Maharg said as he steered Heather toward the one that was right next to Josh.

Struggling to ignore the tawny muscularity of Josh's arms, his taut thighs and lean hips encased in well-worn denims, his magnificent torso under a white knit shirt, Heather took only shallow breaths so she wouldn't be intoxicated by his unique, spicy fragrance. She summoned every ounce of her professionalism and pride. "I understand there's some disagreement about the seating arrangements for the Friday night dinner," she said, deciding to start with that little difficulty and work up to whatever the real problem was.

"That's right," Mrs. Dalrymple said, picking up a slotted cardboard rectangle into which rows of name cards had been slipped to indicate the setup of the enormous table in the main dining room. "Sir Alasdair doesn't seem to think I've followed the proper protocol for the seating order I've chosen. What do you think, dear?"

Heather stared at the chart, then at Mrs. Dalrymple, then at Maharg, and finally back at the seating plan again, her eyes focusing on two names—hers and Josh's, placed side by side.

She leveled a hard gaze at Maharg. His smug little smile confirmed what the chart and Mrs. Dalrymple's exaggerated innocence had suggested. Matchmaking. Obvious, clumsy matchmaking.

She glanced at Josh and was certain he found the whole situation highly entertaining. He was amused, Heather thought as a shaft of fury tore through her. He was *toying* with her!

She felt like throttling all three of them.

Instead, she smiled sweetly. "Well now, I can see that you really do have a serious problem," she said.

Mrs. Dalrymple frowned. "We do?"

Maharg leaned forward to peer at the chart,

though it was upside down so Heather wasn't sure how much he could see. "What problem?" he demanded.

Watching Heather give the chart another close examination, her forehead creased in feigned worry, Josh waited for whatever nonsense she was about to weave. The darkening of her eyes and the shards of emerald that had appeared in them had been ample warning of both her anger and her incorrigible sense of mischief. He didn't blame her for either; he'd never seen two more inept Cupids than Maharg and Mrs. Dalrymple. But their hearts were in the right places. Josh hoped Heather wouldn't lose sight of that fact.

"Well now," she began at last, "I don't know the first thing about protocol, but I do know that you can't put an Armstrong below the salt if the Armstrong's maternal clan is MacDonald, as in this instance, and most particularly when you've a Campbell at the table. It's a custom that goes back to the time of the border reivers, when an Armstrong, an especially fierce fellow descended from the Lords of the Isles, was seated at the far end of the table from his host, who of course was a Campbell."

"Of course," Josh murmured, watching Heather in rapt amazement.

She gave him a fleeting smile, then sobered and went on with her impromptu work of fiction. "Anyway, Armstrong took exception to what he considered a snub and went at Campbell with a claymore, starting a riot that ended with everyone slaughtered and a curse hanging over any table that resembles the one that started all the trouble. Now, in those days, such a melee might have been considered an outstandingly successful party, but I doubt that you'll want to risk it."

"I've never heard that story," Mrs. Dalrymple said, frowning.

"I believe the lass could be right," Maharg said as he scratched his chin thoughtfully. "I seem to recall hearing about that incident as a child."

As Josh saw Heather's lips twitch in a suppressed smile, he knew for certain she was fabricating the entire tale.

She went on to fuss over other seating combinations, making up superstitions and omens out of whole cloth to explain why this or that plan wouldn't work. "And here," she said after decimating the chart, "you've put Alison MacFie with Duncan Robertson. It won't do. It won't do at all."

"Why not?" Maharg thundered impatiently, pounding his stick on the terrace floor. "Surely there's no clan feud or blasted-fool custom or bad-luck talisman connected with those two names."

"Well, it's just that I know a little about the individuals concerned," Heather said blithely. "You see, Miss MacFie is a staunch Democrat, and Mr. Robertson is a Republican favorite son." She smiled as if her explanation were adequate.

"Yes, well, what's wrong with that?" Maharg demanded.

Heather blinked with exaggerated surprise at his lack of sensitivity. "Why, everybody knows what kind of trouble that sort of pairing could lead to." She gave Josh a saccharine smile. "As a fellow American, wouldn't you agree?"

He managed not to chuckle. "Definitely. Never, ever put those two people together. Not even on the same side of the table. Not in the same room, if you can help it."

Both Maharg and Mrs. Dalrymple studied Heather, clearly beginning to suspect what she was up to. But since they also knew what they'd been up to, and therefore understood why she was teasing them, they chose not to question anything she'd said.

Mrs. Dalrymple finally cried uncle. "What on earth are we to do?"

"Finch," Heather said decisively.

"Finch?" Maharg repeated.

Heather nodded. "Finch. He's an expert on protocol. Let him arrange the seating. And as far as the bad omens go—well, I'll look in my book of recipes for curse negators, just to be on the safe side." She smiled reassuringly. "I'm sure we'll be fine. So Finch will re-jig the plan, and there'll be no arguments from anyone. Agreed?"

Though Mrs. Dalrymple nodded immediately, Maharg grumbled that he could remember a time when a laird's word was law and people didn't listen to the ramblings of silly girls. But finally he promised to let Finch be the arbitrator.

Heather drained her glass of lemonade and stood up. "If that's all, then, I'll be on my way."

Josh leapt to his feet. "I'll drive you."

She turned and gave him the iciest glare she could muster. "Thank you, Mr. Campbell, but the bus will be just fine." Without waiting for him to insist, she said a quick good-bye and strode through the French doors, through the ballroom, out to the front door, and down the steps to the driveway.

She was halfway to the road when she heard footsteps behind her. Quickening her pace, she suddenly lurched to a stop as a large hand curled around her upper arm. Heather barely restrained herself from screeching.

Josh gave her a forced smile. "I said I'd drive you home."

Heather returned the smile in kind. "And I said a bus would be fine."

"Don't be childish, dammit," he said, frustrated and annoyed that she was blaming him for other people's foolishness.

"Don't be childish? Why not?" Heather asked, her voice dangerously calm. "After all, that's what I am, isn't it? A child? Isn't that what you think? Just because I'm not prepared to fall all over you, on your terms and only your terms, I'm a naive little girl, right?" With a sudden, surprise move, she shook her arm free of Josh's grasp and started for the road again. "I don't know what your game is, Campbell, but I don't want to play. You come out here and take over *my* friends until *I'm* uncomfortable and feel like an idiot. You let them play at matchmaking, perhaps even put them up to it just to enjoy a little ego stroking, since we both know it isn't because you're the least bit interested in me. That's rotten, Josh Campbell. Really rotten."

Josh couldn't believe that Heather thought he wasn't interested in her. She was on his mind day and night. His body was aching permanently because of her.

But he didn't think the timing was right to say so. "Hey, I was just sitting there minding my own business," he protested instead, surprised at how fast he had to walk to keep up with her. "And I'm not trying to take over your friends. I like these people, okay? Is that allowed? Or are they your private property?"

Heather stopped in her tracks and whirled on him. "Why are you doing all those things around the house? Are you the hired man these days?"

"No, I'm not the hired man. I'm doing those little chores as a . . . a neighborly gesture." Deciding the explanation sounded lame, Josh raked his fingers through his hair, trying to come up with a better one. "I'm doing them because . . ." He heaved an explosive sigh. "Because they need doing, that's why." He couldn't admit to Heather, as he was just beginning to admit to himself, that he kept finding excuses to spend time at Maharg's because of her, because it was the only way he could count on seeing her. "What do you think my reason is?" he asked more quietly, putting the ball back in Heather's court.

She stared at him, trying to make herself believe Josh had some ulterior motive for his kindness toward Maharg. But she couldn't. For some reason she didn't begin to understand, she knew Josh was helping Maharg out of the goodness of his heart. "Because they need doing," she said at last, her shoulders sagging. "Let's not fight, Josh. I just want to go home, okay? On the bus. It shouldn't be too much to ask." She turned to walk away.

"You owe me a dinner," Josh said out of sheer desperation. "Tonight seems like a good time to have it, given that Mrs. Dalrymple didn't stuff us with sandwiches and cakes for a change." He didn't bother mentioning that he'd suggested to the housekeeper that he wouldn't mind taking Heather out somewhere for a bite, if she happened to be hungry.

Heather quickened her pace, panicking.

"Are you going to welsh on me?" he asked.

Heather stopped, but didn't turn to look at him. "Why are you doing this, Josh?" she asked, her voice suddenly husky. "Why don't you just let me go?"

"Because I can't, Muffin," he said softly. "Because I . . . I just can't."

* * *

Heather sat opposite Josh at a small table beneath the stained-glass window of a venerable downtown pub, loading her fish and chips with malt vinegar and salt, then tucking into them with her usual gusto. No matter how troubled she was, her appetite rarely seemed to be affected. If anything, she ate more heartily when she was upset. "You seem to be giving Maharg a new lease on life," she said after a long, awkward silence.

"You did that before I arrived on the scene, Heather," Josh answered absently. It had just occurred to him that he'd reverted to one of his more manipulative habits, choosing a pub in his neighborhood, close to his apartment. It was the kind of trick he'd learned early in life. When a woman seemed willing, why give her passion time to cool off during a long drive to someplace private?

All of a sudden he didn't think very highly of the Josh Campbell who'd done that sort of thing.

"Maybe you're just a nice guy," Heather commented, still puzzling over all the chores Josh had been doing for Maharg with no apparent reward except friendship and perhaps a bit of gratitude.

"A nice guy?" Josh repeated with a little snort of derision. "You've said that before. And as I think I've suggested before, I'm the kind of guy your mother warned you about."

Heather laughed. "She never warned me about anybody except headhunters, so unless you have a collection of those awful little shrunken skulls, I probably can look after myself, even with you."

One of the things Josh liked best about Heather was her cheekiness. And the fact that some of the outrageous things she said were true. Remembering that she'd mentioned living in some very remote regions with unbelievably primitive tribes, he was prepared to believe she feared very little.

Perhaps, he thought, as he'd thought so many times since meeting her, she *should* be more wary. "I don't have shrunken skulls on my bookshelves," he said, "but where women are concerned, a head-hunter just about describes me."

"Why do you do that?" Heather asked, spearing a french fry and tasting it with the grave attention of a fussy gourmet.

"Why do I do what?" Josh asked as he picked at his steak-and-kidney pie. "Act like a headhunter?"

Frowning, Heather added another generous sprinkling of salt and vinegar to her plate. What she'd been asking was why he was so hard on himself. But now that he'd mentioned it, she did wonder why he acted like a headhunter. She didn't believe he wanted to.

"You're a nutritionist's nightmare," Josh commented.

"Don't worry about me," she said with a bright smile. She picked up her glass tankard of dark, foaming beer and raised it in a toast. "This magic elixir not only washes everything down, it cancels out all the bad effects of any food."

He shook his head in mock despair. "Where did you ever hear a theory like that?"

"I didn't hear it. I made it up." Heather paused. She was more comfortable arguing with Josh about nonsense than trying to deal with the more troubling undercurrents between them. Yet in the next instant she heard herself barreling ahead. "Why do you keep warning me about yourself? I admit you can be a pain, but basically you don't seem like such a bad fellow to me. What's your secret sin?"

"No real sin, I suppose," Josh answered. "It's

just that the background I've had doesn't make for the kind of niceness I think you're talking about. And looking for."

Heather stabbed a fry with such vehemence, Josh winced. "Let's get something straight," she said as she glared across the table at him. "I'm not looking for any special qualities in a man, for the simple reason that I'm not looking for a man. Would you like to know why *I* think you issue your warnings?"

"I'm not sure I'd like it, but I'm curious," Josh answered. "Shoot."

"I think you want to shift responsibility to me by telling me up front that you're a cad. If the old sparks between us flare up again and something happens, I'll have no cause for complaint when you walk away in the morning without a backward glance."

"You're pretty cynical for a—" He stopped short.

But Heather had no problem supplying the rest. "For a little girl," she supplied sweetly, then pushed her plate toward him. "You know, I've often wondered about cynicism. Was the boy who said the emperor was naked a cynic? Or were the actual cynics the tailors who sold the emperor a bill of nongoods? Or was the emperor the ultimate in cynicism for allowing himself to believe what made him feel good for the moment?" She smiled again. "Try the fries. They're fabulous."

Josh accepted the offer, only vaguely aware of what he was doing. He was in a state of semishock. Sweet, playful, vulnerable Heather was more than a match for any headhunter.

Noticing a lean, darkly attractive Scotsman entering the pub—a friend of one of the *Dreamweavers* tour guides who lived in this part of the city—Heather waved and smiled. "Hi, Sandy," she called.

Josh followed the direction of Heather's glance and was shocked by a stab of jealousy—an emotion that had become part of him only since he'd met her. Not a single night had gone by in three weeks that he hadn't wondered whether she was with some other man. He'd never felt that way about anyone. Not in his entire life.

Once again, Heather turned her smile to Josh. "What kind of background were you talking about when you said it didn't make for niceness? The rough-and-ready ambience of an oil rig?"

"Partly that," Josh said guardedly, beginning to take more care with the way he talked to Heather. She wouldn't put up with being patronized. And he realized that his pet defense against any woman who might get under his skin was to be annoyingly patronizing. "It's more a case of having lived in a man's world since I was a little kid," he went on, strangely eager to explain himself to Heather. "My mother ran off with her lover when I was ten, and I haven't seen her since. My opinion of females wasn't, shall we say, enhanced," he admitted with a wry smile. "As it happened, there were no surrogates around. No cookie-baking grannies, no kindly aunts or casserole-bearing neighbors. I went to boys' schools. I tinkered with cars and hung around my father's dive shop on a Fort Lauderdale fishing dock. The supposedly softening feminine influence was missing completely from my upbringing, Heather. Completely."

Heather realized with surprise that Josh's ironic manner was a facade. Growing up as he had, he'd bought into the archaic idea that it wasn't manly to talk of old emotional wounds. But she'd seen a glimpse of the vulnerable human under his invincible surface, and it tugged at her heart. "Didn't your father ever fall in love with anyone else?" she asked quietly.

Josh shook his head. "A fishing dock doesn't attract a lot of unattached ladies. And Pop had been burned badly. He hit the bottle after my mother left. Fortunately, he had a buddy who helped keep the dive shop going until Pop pulled himself together." Absently, Josh snitched another fry from Heather's plate. "That shop became Dad's life, at least until he retired a couple of years ago. He spent almost all his time there, chatting up cronies and tourists, reliving and embellishing the diving experiences of his youth until he started seeing himself almost as an unsung Jacques Cousteau." Josh dreaded the possibility of ending up the same way. He refused to think about it. "As far as women were concerned—well, to put it bluntly, when Pop needed one, he paid by the hour."

"What about you?" Heather asked. "Didn't you start meeting girls? Liking them?"

Josh shook his head and shrugged. "I grew up seeing females as commodities at best, nuisances at worst. Okay, I didn't like the idea of paying for feminine companionship, so I didn't follow my father's example. Instead, I learned to be passably charming. Enough to get what I'm looking for, which until lately has been mainly a few hours of pleasure."

"Until lately?" Heather repeated, not sure what Josh was trying to say—or not to say—with that telling phrase.

Josh realized only then what he'd blurted out. He frowned and took another fry.

Sensing that Josh longed for more from life than his wariness would permit him to accept,

Heather found herself wanting to hold him as much as to be held by him, to try to kiss away the hurt of the ten-year-old boy who still lurked angrily inside him.

The unquenchable desire Heather hadn't stopped feeling for Josh suddenly took on added depth. She was tempted to accept whatever he would give her, on any terms he chose to offer. And to give him whatever he wanted and needed, no strings attached.

But she stopped herself before she could do or say anything foolishly impulsive. For her, making love to Josh wouldn't be something she could get over easily when he inevitably walked away. And as for his needs—there were other, stronger women around who could tend the psychic scars left by his runaway mother, Heather told herself, though the thought made her almost physically ill. "Aren't these things great?" she asked for want of another distraction.

Josh gave his head a little shake. He had no idea what Heather was talking about. Something soft and hypnotic in her deep green eyes had a way of clearing his mind, like a powerful magnet erasing a videotape. "Great?" he repeated, finally realizing she was referring to the food. Only then did he notice that he'd demolished most of her fries. He nodded, managing a smile. "Yeah. They're great. I've always liked fries with my salt and vinegar."

Heather moved her plate toward him again. "Have the rest. I'm full."

But Josh stared unseeingly at the plate, his body and spirit suddenly aching with a new kind of hunger, one no mere food could satisfy. One no mere night of pleasure could assuage.

"I think we should go," Heather said, panicking

and not sure why. She reached for the check the waiter had left on the table, but Josh got to it first. "That's not fair," she said without smiling. It was important to her to pay for the modest little supper. Her sense of independence was under siege, and every small act to protect it was vital. "After all the rides you've given me, and the sandals . . ."

"Would you forget the sandals?" Josh said with exasperated amusement. But an idea came to him. Not ready yet to give up on the evening, he glanced at the corner behind the bar and saw a way to keep things going for a while. "Tell you what, Muffin. I challenge you to a dart match. The winner pays the bill."

"The *winner* pays?" Heather asked, a tiny grin curving her lips. Her competitive nature was aroused—and the truth was, she couldn't resist the chance to be with Josh a little longer.

"What do you say?" Josh persisted.

Heather shrugged. "Okay, Campbell. You're on."

As they picked up their tankards of beer and went to the dart board, Josh set out the terms, vaguely thinking that Heather had accepted the challenge too easily. "Two out of three, standard rules, start with five hundred and one?" He half-expected Heather to ask what he meant.

But she surprised him. "Fine," she answered, choosing red darts while Josh picked green.

"By the way," he said with a teasing grin as he put their names on the chalkboard, "I probably should have mentioned that I'm the unofficial dart champion of the North Sea."

"Really? How impressive," Heather said, taking her place at the line to make the opening toss that, along with Josh's, would determine by closeness to the bull's-eye who would get first throw in the game.

Busy admiring Heather's lithe form and long, shapely legs, Josh almost didn't bother looking to see where her dart had landed. When he did spare the board a glance while taking a sip of beer, he choked. She'd hit the bull's-eye. Dead center.

"By the way," Heather said with her most angelic smile, "I probably should have mentioned—I'm the unofficial dart champion of the *South* Seas."

Eight

At the end of the first two games the match was a draw, and several of the pub's other patrons had started gathering around the small dart-playing area, attracted by the unusual expertise of the two opponents.

As Josh erased the scores from the chalkboard, Heather removed her jacket, deciding it restricted her freedom of movement. Besides, the room was starting to feel sultry. Every time Josh happened to brush against her or look at her in a certain way, the warmth seemed to close in on her.

Josh turned from the chalkboard, and Heather immediately regretted having taken off her jacket; his intense gaze was like a searing brand that made the tips of her breasts harden and protrude through her thin cotton shell. As she assumed her throwing stance, Heather felt a flush stealing over her breasts and throat.

Captivated by the evidence that Heather wasn't as immune to him as she liked to pretend, Josh closely watched her every move, aching to touch her soft breasts and take their swollen nipples in his mouth. He wanted to press his lips to the vulnerable pulse spot just under her jawline that was throbbing visibly and wildly. He wanted to whisk her away to explore her sweet, eager femininity at his leisure.

She took aim for her throw, absently running the tip of her tongue over her lips.

Her gesture affected Josh like a jolt of electricity. He grabbed his tankard, curled his fingers tightly around the handle, and took a long pull of beer that did little to cool him down. The solitude of his apartment beckoned as he watched the fluid movements of Heather's body, the long gentle curve of her flanks when she leaned into the throw, the straining of her breasts against her blouse.

His inattention to the darts made Josh miss the necessary opening double when it was time for his first round, so Heather took an early lead. Then, moving into place for his second set of throws, he caught a whiff of Heather's light, rich perfume, and he managed only to get into the game; he didn't come close to catching up.

Only when Heather seemed to fall prey to the same kind of distraction, her breasts rising and falling as if she were gasping for air, her hands shaking so her shots didn't quite hit their marks, did Josh decide that someone would have to concentrate on the game or they would be at it all night. And he had far more interesting ideas for whiling away the remainder of the evening with Heather Sinclair than playing darts in a pub. She wanted him as much as he wanted her—so why the defensive little courting dance they'd been performing for three weeks?

Pulling himself together, Josh managed a triple fifteen and a double nineteen, putting him back in the running. The onlookers applauded noisily, their interest renewed.

"Terrific shots," Heather said graciously, swallowing hard as she moved to the throwing line, beginning to wish she hadn't accepted Josh's challenge after all. The more she watched his controlled power and easy male grace, the more he excited her.

Nevertheless, plagued by his warnings about the kind of man he was, she found that winning the match was becoming vital to her, a symbol that somehow she would resist joining the apparent legion of Josh Campbell's cast-off women.

"Come on, Heather," she heard from someone in the crowd. Turning, she saw Sandy playing cheerleader. She wasn't surprised; the man was a notorious flirt who'd come on to her a few times before. She grinned, almost wishing she were attracted to him, rather surprised he left her cold. He had the good looks and unthreatening kind of maleness she far preferred to Josh's surfeit of masculinity.

"You can win," Sandy said. "Do it, lass."

Checking out Heather's chief supporter, Josh met Sandy's gaze; the defiantly predatory expression in the Scotsman's eyes was unmistakable.

Josh scowled. Heather hadn't been at all flustered when Sandy had entered the bar, and hadn't so much as glanced at him again until he'd made this pitch for her attention. But was she interested? Could they be involved with each other?

Something twisted Josh's insides. Jealousy again, he thought, still hardly believing he was capable of it. It wasn't supposed to be part of his deliberately limited emotional repertoire.

The match became a background blur to Josh as he stared at Heather, slowly coming to terms with the incredible realization that she'd managed —without even trying—to slip right past all his defenses and make him feel things he'd never felt before, had never wanted to feel.

As he heard a cheer go up, he blinked, belatedly looked at the dart board, and saw that Heather had taken another leap forward in points, putting her well in the lead. With renewed interest, he watched her prepare for her third shot. She was just letting go when a familiar feminine voice said, "Josh, how nice! I was hopin' you'd be here tonight!"

At the exact moment that Heather released her missile, she turned her head, startled and curious, wondering who the woman was who had the melodious tone and who was obviously familiar with Josh.

"Maggie," Josh said with surprise, pleasure, and a touch of chagrin. He wasn't sure he was ready for his closest friends to meet Heather yet. Not when he was just beginning to grasp what the girl might come to mean to him, and not when Maggie's matchmaking urges were as strong as Maharg's, if more subtle.

It occurred to Josh that he should have anticipated the possibility of running into Maggie and Donald Alexander; they lived in his neighborhood and frequented the same pub he did.

As she watched the fond embrace shared by Josh and Maggie, Heather felt a tight knot form in her stomach. Her quick glance took in Maggie's snug jeans, an open windbreaker of expensively stylish, gray stone-washed denim, and a red T-shirt that emphasized her graceful curves as well as her rose-touched, creamy complexion. In perhaps her late twenties, Maggie was dauntingly lovely, with her smooth, shoulder-length black hair,

midnight-blue eyes, and an aura of poise and so-
phistication that made Heather feel like an awkward adolescent.

Suddenly Heather forgot that Josh wasn't her
fabled Right Man, that in fact, he was, by his own
harsh description, very much the Wrong Man. All
she could think of was that Maggie would know
how to please a man like Josh Campbell. Maggie
wouldn't do anything as tomboyish as giving him
a run for his money at darts for the dubious
privilege of paying the evening's bill. Maggie
wouldn't act like a man's buddy, and she un-
doubtedly had no qualms whatsoever about being
swept off her feet by a masterful Viking raider.

Maggie, Heather thought miserably, was a woman,
not a little girl.

Belatedly, Josh realized that Heather and Maggie
were sizing each other up with a thoroughness
that had added a whole new drama to interest the
onlookers. In no mood to provide an impromptu
soap opera, he spoke in clipped tones, trying to
get everyone back on track. "Take your shot again,
Heather. You were distracted."

"No," she answered firmly, tearing her glance
from Maggie long enough to give Josh a forced
smile. "It's part of the game not to be distracted."

"Take a wee gander, folks," Sandy piped up, his
gaze meeting Josh's glance with a brief but direct
challenge, then moving on to Heather, his eyes
alight with glee as he pointed with his thumb
toward the dart board.

Josh couldn't help joining the hearty laughter
that broke out. Heather had scored a triple twenty.
"Good for you, Muffin," he said, surprised by the
rush of affection and pride that surged through
him.

Heather was confused. Even as Josh's unexpectedly fond manner warmed her, she was irritated by his use of the nickname she'd previously liked. Would he call his other women *Muffin*? Would he give Maggie such a juvenile nickname? Not bloody likely! No doubt he'd used it on purpose as a signal to Maggie that the reddish-haired hoyden he was amusing himself with was nothing to worry about.

"Where's Donald?" Josh asked as Heather yanked out darts and noisily rattled the chalkboard, slashing a line through her previous score, subtracting sixty points as she wrote down her new total.

Heather's mild burst of temper immediately subsided. Donald?

"He's runnin' an errand at the little shop across the street," Maggie said. "It's what we came out for, but we thought we'd stop in here for a pint." She watched Heather retire to the sidelines to chugalug half her beer. "I see you're on the verge of giving this brute the trouncing he deserves, Heather," she said with a grin. "Please carry on, won't you?"

Heather put down her mug, drew the back of her hand over her mouth to be sure she hadn't left a foam mustache, and felt a great wave of relief wash over her. Maggie was part of a couple. She wasn't a Viking's prize after all. She was with someone named Donald, probably a dear, gentle, professorial type, the kind real-life women like Maggie were drawn to.

Forcefully reminding herself that Josh could have all the ladies in Edinburgh on a string for all she cared, and the ones in Glasgow and Inverness and Aberdeen as well, Heather smiled at Maggie. "I really ought to thank you for distracting me on that shot," she said with a wink. "I would have been happy with a straight twenty."

Maggie chuckled. "A ferlie must have helped guide the dart to the triple."

"Could be," Heather said, beginning to think she could learn to like Maggie. "Of course, I saw three crows sitting in a row on a fence this morning. You can't beat that kind of luck, now can you?"

"I should say not," Maggie agreed enthusiastically.

Josh was amazed by the instant rapport between the two women. "What's a ferlie?" he asked, trying to stay in the social game, if not in the dart match.

"A ferlie is anything out of the ordinary," Maggie explained, adding a conspiratorial glance at Heather, "from the Loch Ness monster to the likes of you, Josh Campbell. But in this case I meant a helpful wee ghost, probably female. Now, hadn't you better get busy and see if you can redeem your precious male pride?"

Heather laughed quietly, deciding that she indeed liked Maggie very much.

As Josh stepped into place, a delayed realization hit him: Heather had been jealous. What shocked him most was that he was pleased. The old Josh had bristled at the slightest hint of a lady's possessiveness, but he was beginning to understand that where Heather Sinclair was concerned, none of his former ways or rules applied.

He finished his three tosses and added up his score.

"Well, you're startin' to catch up a bit," Maggie said with sweet condescension, giving Heather a thumbs-up sign.

It amused Josh that Heather and Maggie seemed to have formed a strange sort of feminine bond that left him bumbling around in typical mascu-

line confusion. He wasn't needed even for intro-
ductions; the ladies had bypassed such trivial
formalities. But when Maggie's husband finally
wandered into the pub, Josh called a time-out.
"Heather, I want you to meet Donald Alexander,
Maggie's husband," he said, adding to Donald,
"I'm glad you're here, pal. I need an ally against
these females and their battalion of supernatural
helpers." He signaled to the waitress for beers for
Donald and Maggie in the universal way: holding
up two fingers and pointing first to the couple,
then to his own beer mug.

Taken aback, Heather stared at the two men.
Dressed in worn jeans and a gray sweatshirt, Donald Alexander was every bit as tall and muscular
as Josh, and almost as attractive, his hair an
unruly tumble of russet, his eyes a penetrating
blue, his features roughly blasted out of granite
but softened by what appeared to be a permanent
devilish grin. He wasn't the mild-mannered-professor
type at all.

For a brief moment, before telling herself she
was being ridiculous, Heather felt she'd lost Maggie
as an ally in their us-against-them game, since
the woman obviously had fallen for a Josh Campbell clone.

Donald glanced at the score on the chalkboard.
"So it's another Battle of the Sexes, is it?" he said
with a mischievous glint in his eyes. "We seem to
have to teach the lassies the same old lessons over
and over again, Josh, though at the moment you
don't seem to be doin' a great job of it." Laughing
heartily, Donald clapped Josh on the back and
added, "The pride of all manhood rests with you,
lad. Don't let us down, or there'll be no livin' with
our women."

Privately, Josh got a kick out of the extra edge

Donald's challenge added to the game. And, amazingly, he liked the ring of Donald's phrase. *Our women.* The day was full of surprises. But with a pretense of being disgruntled about the pressure Donald had put on him, Josh grumbled, "Just what I needed, buddy. A bracing pep talk."

"It's just what *I* needed," Heather said firmly as she took her place at the throwing line. *Our women,* she repeated silently. Ignoring the small explosions of unbidden excitement the phrase detonated within her, she renewed her longtime resolve that Heather Sinclair would be no one's woman but her own. Ever. Though she smiled along with the others, Heather was driven to a serious battle for supremacy. "I've been complacent about this match, but now . . ."

"Right, lass," Maggie said. "Put these chest-beatin' gorillas in their place."

Immediately, the audience was sharply divided, the women cheering for Heather, the men backing Josh, and with every new arrival who came through the open pub door, the ranks on each side swelled.

Josh noted that only Sandy was the holdout among the men. Though Sandy remained quiet, it was clear by the direction of his steady, dark gaze which player had his vote.

Heather took aim carefully, her allegiance to her sex temporarily curing her of her lovesick malaise. She grinned as she hit another triple twenty, earning a great cry from the ladies. Her next two throws were good. One more round was all she needed.

As Heather stepped to the sidelines, Josh winked at her and took her place in front of the dart board, the tiny gesture meant partly to remind her that the game was all in fun, but mainly as a back-off message to Sandy.

Among all the other atavistic instincts Heather seemed to arouse in him, Josh mused with an inner smile, it seemed he could include fierce male territorialism.

"I guess I'd better make this round the last," he said teasingly. His score was one-sixteen. It was theoretically possible for him to go out on three darts, though chancy: Two bull's-eyes at fifty points each, plus a double eight, would do the job nicely. But two bull's-eyes would be pretty tricky to get, so Josh refigured his options and decided to try for another combination.

He threw the first dart. Not bad, he decided as several of the men triumphantly pounded their pints on nearby tables; a triple eighteen was exactly what he'd wanted.

"You're almost there, lad!" one of his supporters called out. "Try for a double twenty!"

Josh grinned. "Just what I had in mind," he said as he took aim for his second throw. When it hit the mark, the men in the pub nearly brought down the roof.

Maggie leaned toward Heather and smiled. "Josh tends to put his whole heart into everything he does."

Heather smiled back but felt a slight chill inside her. By Josh's own testimony, there were some pursuits into which he put everything except his heart.

Heather's own heart was making its presence felt, however, pounding so hard, she thought it must be audible. No matter how hard she tried, she couldn't suppress her powerful response to the man.

Josh needed only a double eleven to go out.

Heather held her breath as he threw, appalled to find herself almost rooting for him, traitor that she was.

Josh wanted to win, if only to get the game over with. He was getting a bit weary of being the pub's main attraction, and he wanted to have a quick beer with Maggie and Donald, then steal away with Heather.

But his third dart landed just outside the double zone, netting him only a straight eleven.

Though his supporters collectively groaned in disappointment, they applauded his effort.

As Heather went to the line again, several combinations of numbers were tossed at her from her supporters, all adding up to what she needed to win—a mere sixty-one points. It was a do-or-die situation, because Josh wouldn't need more than another round to get the eleven he still had left.

She aimed for a triple seven, deciding to get the odd number out of the way. The dart sailed straight to its mark.

"Good shot," Josh said, his voice quietly deep amid all the feminine hoots of excitement.

It was odd, Heather thought as her heart beat faster, how Josh's approval could give her an inner glow such as none of the lusty cheers from the others could inspire. She smiled at him, then took a deep breath, sharply reminding herself not to go soft at this point. She had a game to win, and she was almost there.

But she couldn't tear her gaze from his, and couldn't shake the increasing sense of being in a microcosmic world with Josh, only Josh, while everyone else in the room receded to a vague mass, like an audience beyond the footlights in a darkened theater. She was in the grip of the strange, galvanized connection with Josh Campbell that she'd been battling for the past three weeks. Only three weeks, she thought with astonishment. Surely she'd known Josh much, much longer.

"Don't lose your nerve now," a male voice said to her. "Get that double twenty, lass."

Josh's eyes narrowed. Damned Sandy again, he thought, wishing his own claim on Heather were more solid so he could tell the Scot to go find his own woman.

Heather took aim, hesitated for just an instant, then let her second dart fly. The dart landed just beyond the outer wire, scoring nothing. No matter, she told herself. She still had another chance to make the same throw.

She could taste victory as she readied herself for the shot; she wasn't likely to miss twice.

Then, without warning, pandemonium broke out. Just as Heather had gotten a bead on her mark, she heard a fast clicking sound behind her on the wooden floor of the pub. The instant that she let go of the dart, she felt something large and furry sideswipe her with such force, she'd have been knocked head over heels but for Josh's lightning-quick move to catch her with one outstretched arm, while using his other arm to fend off what looked like a small, cinnamon-colored bear.

Jumping into the fray, Maggie helped steady Heather as the creature muscled both women aside in a determined battle to give Josh a sloppy, loving embrace. "MacBeth, I thought I sent you home!" Maggie scolded. She heard her husband's rich laughter filling the pub and she whirled on him. "Don, for mercy's sake, get that rampagin' cur off Josh, will you?" She shook her head furiously. "Och, I wish your owner would put you on a good stout leash, you ridiculous mongrel," she added, not making it clear whether she was referring to the dog or Donald.

Falling back against a pillar, Heather watched the fracas in stunned silence for a moment.

"Okay, MacBeth, that's . . . that's enough," Josh was saying as he shielded his face from the sloppy kisses the beast was trying to bestow, its tongue lolling out and its huge, liquid eyes filled with adoration.

The poor thing was as besotted with Josh as she was, though perhaps a trifle more obvious about it, Heather thought, her mouth twitching with amusement.

"MacBeth, this is not *cute*!" Maggie cried, tugging on the dog's floppy ears.

All at once the tension that had been building in Heather for the past three weeks snapped. She started to giggle, then began laughing helplessly, finally lapsing into convulsions of mirth that rolled up from deep inside her until she was bent over double, tears rolling down her cheeks.

"C'mon, Muffin," Josh managed to protest as he struggled to extricate himself. "It's not *that* hilarious!"

"Och, but it is," Heather said with difficulty. "I knew you were a heartbreaker, Campbell, but I'd no idea of the scope of your conquests."

There was that lilt of hers again, Josh thought, wishing he could ditch MacBeth and haul Heather into his arms instead.

At last Donald decided to pitch in, and soon MacBeth had been coaxed down onto all fours.

"I'm sorry, Heather," Josh said when calm had been restored. "Difficult as it must be to believe, I haven't arranged for these little dramas. I think the only honorable solution is for me to concede the game—though I do insist on paying for supper. Given the circumstances, all bets are off. But you've more than proven that the South Seas champion has whipped the North Sea contender all hollow."

The women cheered lustily, and the men booed.

"Not a chance," Heather said adamantly, slowly pulling herself together, glancing into a mirror on a far wall to make sure her mascara was as waterproof as advertised. It was. Finally, she remembered to look at the target. The ferlie had fallen down on the job this time, she thought with a recurring giggle; her third shot had gone right off the board. "As I believe I made clear earlier," she said with as much dignity as she could recapture, "whatever happens is the luck of the game. But you will *not* pay for supper, because I might well have won with that shot."

Donald turned to Maggie with a scowl. "The *winner* pays?"

She shrugged. "I'll never understand Yanks."

Realizing that there was no point arguing with Heather, especially when she was being patently unreasonable, Josh suggested a compromise. "Then you have to take another throw."

Heather set her jaw. "Do you think my sisters conceded any games on the *Dreamweaver* just because a typhoon suddenly blew up and made the boat list to one side just as someone was throwing? No, sir. I play for keeps, Campbell, come what may."

The men roared their approval while the women good-naturedly jeered.

Josh grew serious, gazing at Heather for a long moment. He'd known from the start that she was the kind of woman who would play only for keeps. It was exactly what had been scaring him off. But suddenly he wasn't as leery as he'd always felt he should be. "Maybe that's how I want to play too," he said, moving to stand close to her, his hands resting loosely on his hips as he looked down at her and spoke very softly so no one but Heather could hear. "And maybe I won't accept a false victory." Until he'd said the words, Josh hadn't fully grasped that seducing Heather could never be enough for him; he wanted to share much, much more than passing physical pleasure with her.

Something in Josh's tone made Heather quiver inside. She knew he wasn't talking about the dart game any longer. "I'll make a bargain with you," she said, her voice as low as his. She tried to keep her manner light and bantering, not ready for the change she sensed in Josh. "If you feel so terrible about winning because of MacBeth, we can call the game a draw. But I'll pay for supper."

"Some bargain," Josh said with a shake of his head. "Here's the way it has to be, Heather: One shot each, the closest to the bull's-eye is declared champ. Winner take all."

"All?" Heather repeated warily. What else did Josh have up his sleeve?

He grinned, his hazel eyes glinting as he put forth his proposal. "You saw by the infamous seating plan that Maharg has asked me to take part in his clan gathering. Apart from his matchmaking efforts, I think he likes the idea of tossing in a Campbell among all those MacDonald relatives of his. So here are the stakes, Heather: If I win this throw, I not only cover tonight's tab, I go to the Friday night dinner and ball as your official escort."

Heather stared at him, her heartbeat doing flips and cartwheels. Josh wanted to take her to the ball? She felt like Cinderella when the prince walked in with her glass slipper.

"On with the game!" someone shouted.

Josh was sure the voice was Sandy's. Narrowing his eyes, he held Heather's gaze. "Well, Muffin?"

"What if I win?" she asked in a strained voice.

Josh grinned. "I guess you get to pay the bill and choose your escort."

Heather couldn't help smiling. The man was impossibly appealing. "All right, Campbell. You're on. Who throws first?"

"The lady, of course," Josh said with a courtly little bow.

Nodding, Heather took her place in front of the board, tried to muster a will to win—despite the intriguing penalty for losing—aimed, and felt her stomach contract with disappointment when she saw her dart go straight to the bull's-eye.

Donald walked up to the board and peered closely at it, then removed the dart and took out a pen to put an ink mark on the hole. "She's a wee bit off the center," he said with a wicked chuckle. "Now's your chance to show what you're made of, Josh."

Josh rolled his eyes. "Thanks again, pal." But for some reason, he had a sudden feeling of confidence. He couldn't lose. He had his own ferlies on his side. Standing at the throwing line, he adjusted the dart in his fingers until its weight felt just right, then made the throw.

Heather's pulse went wild as Josh's dart hit the bull's-eye. She waited, barely able to breathe while Donald went to examine the board. He turned to Heather. "Maybe you'll want to have a look for yourself," he suggested.

She shook her head. "I trust your judgment."

Donald smiled approvingly at her. "This dart hit dead center," he said. "Good lad, Josh!" he added in his great, booming voice as he applauded enthusiastically. "Thanks to Josh Campbell, we men are safe from the dreaded matriarchy for another day!"

Maggie shot her husband a menacing look. "Don't count on it, pet." She turned to Heather with a grin and a wink. "Let the foolish lads crow all they like, Heather. Everyone knows who the evenin's winner really is."

Putting his arm around Heather's shoulders to head for a booth with Maggie and Donald, Josh smiled, fully agreeing with Maggie.

He knew who the evening's winner really was.

Nine

Josh bypassed the street that led to his apartment, taking Heather to her own place instead. Though his burning need to make love to her hadn't abated, a greater force seemed to have taken control of him.

Besides, he thought with a smile, he was enjoying Heather's relaxed, bright chattiness, so refreshing after the stilted conversations they'd had recently.

"It's hard to believe," she said, referring to an exchange she'd heard between Josh and Donald about Maharg's cars. "Were you and Donald serious? Could some old jalopy really command twenty-five thousand dollars?"

Josh laughed. "Calling a '47 Daimler an old jalopy is akin to calling a Ming vase an old pot. But yes, that car, in top shape, could be worth easily that much. And Maharg's vehicles are all in mint condition."

"Do you think he would sell?" Heather asked. "Heaven knows, that kind of money could be a real shot in the arm for his estate, but is he reluctant? Sentimental?"

"Maharg is a canny Scot," Josh said with a chuckle. "He'll sell, though he doesn't want to handle the details himself, and he won't put 'the old dears,' as he calls his cars, on some local dealer's auction block." Josh paused, not sure how Heather would react to his next bit of information. She already suspected his motives for spending so much time helping out at Maharg's place. But she had to be told, so now seemed as good a time as any. "Maharg has asked me to take care of the sales," he said at last, then found himself holding his breath.

Heather turned to stare at Josh. "Why, of course! What a terrific idea!" she said with genuine enthusiasm. "I trust Maharg expects you to collect the going commission."

"As a matter of fact, he does," Josh answered, relieved by Heather's response. After neglecting to mention to her that the matter of selling the cars had come up only a couple of days before—long after he'd started doing odd jobs around the estate—he wouldn't have been surprised if she'd jumped to the wrong conclusion. He wondered why he'd set her up that way. Had he been testing? Suspecting so, he vowed to put an end to that kind of subtle baiting.

Nevertheless, he was pleased that Heather hadn't looked for ulterior motives, and when she began questioning him with obvious eagerness about how he would find buyers, negotiate prices, and take care of countless business details he hadn't even thought of yet, he discovered that a seed of excitement was taking root inside him, an embryonic confidence and zest for the future that he hadn't felt for a long, long time.

As they approached Heather's village, a familiar, awkward silence fell between them.

"Maggie and Donald are super," Heather said, her voice suddenly strained.

"That they are," Josh said absently.

"So Maggie helped you get back on your feet after you'd been injured in the oil-rig explosion?" Heather went on, determined to chat as if she weren't tense about what might happen when they reached her house. "She must be a wonderful physiotherapist."

Blinking, Josh forced himself to call a halt to the erotic images that had begun appearing in his mind. "Who?" he asked, his expression vague.

"Maggie," Heather answered. "I said she must be a wonderful physiotherapist."

Josh chuckled. "If being a ruthless sadist is what makes a wonderful therapist, Maggie's the best."

"Were you a difficult patient?"

"Awful. I bellyached constantly."

"But according to Maggie, you practically willed yourself back onto your feet even after there was a good chance you might never walk again. So you must have had some saving graces."

Josh glanced at Heather, raising one thick blond brow. "At what point did Maggie manage to confide all that?"

"It was when you and Donald were talking about some soccer match," Heather said. "Maggie admires you tremendously, you know. And for some reason she seemed to want me to understand how determined you can be when you go after something." Even as she spoke, Heather wondered why she would make such a leading, provocative remark.

Josh smiled, but kept his eyes on the road as he turned the car onto Heather's street. "Does my determination worry you, Heather?" He paused, then added softly, "Considering that you seem to have wandered into my sights?"

Heather hesitated. His determination was exactly what bothered her. Falling for such a man would be like negotiating the ocean in a rowboat; a person could get swamped. "A little," she answered after a moment. She remembered what harmless fun it had seemed to imagine Josh as a Norse invader about to carry her off to some sensual Valhalla. And there had been moments during this very evening when she'd felt ready to go anywhere with Josh if he'd so much as crooked his finger in invitation. Her body was still simmering with the heat he'd aroused in her. But dealing with a fantasy that threatened to become reality within minutes was a whole other matter.

Without another word, Josh pulled into the parking lot at the end of the street, switched off the ignition, got out to walk around to Heather's side, and helped her from the car. Putting his arm around her shoulders, he held her tucked against his side as they walked to her house.

Reaching the door, Josh tried the knob, then shook his head in frustration as the door opened. "Dammit, Muffin, I wish you would lock up your place," he scolded. "I don't care how peaceful a neighborhood this is, do you have to be so infernally trusting?"

As Heather started to enter the cottage, Josh caught her elbow and pulled her back. "Let me go in first."

She gave him a bemused smile as she followed him inside. "Your protectiveness is lovely, Josh, but I've been taking care of myself for quite a while. Anyway, you can see that I've left a light on. I always do."

"Not good enough," Josh said, then suddenly realized how presumptuous he was being. Just outside the living room archway, he turned and drew Heather into his arms. "I do have a tendency to overstep myself," he said quietly, brushing light kisses over her temple and forehead. "You seem to bring out instincts in me I'm not sure how to handle."

His uncertainty disarmed Heather. "I'm having a little trouble handling my instincts too," she admitted, relaxing against him.

"We're quite the pair, you and I," Josh murmured, stroking her hair, her shoulders, her long, slender back. "As wary as a couple of lost desert travelers seeing an oasis and wondering if it's a mirage."

Surprised that Josh felt doubts so like her own, Heather smiled but didn't answer, burying her face in the warmth of his neck, allowing her body to fit itself to his, her curves yielding to his hard planes, her taut nerves and muscles letting go as his strong hands lightly massaged her back. She breathed deeply, and as she inhaled the clean spiciness of his scent, she felt half-drugged, unable to think, merely feeling, responding, wanting. Surrendering to temptation, she grazed her lips over the underside of Josh's jawline, then retraced the trail with the tip of her tongue, reveling in the delicious taste of his skin, the quick intake of his breath, the sudden, rigid heat of his body against hers.

Josh had intended to kiss Heather good night at her door. He wanted to take time to know her, to dispel some of her doubts—and his own. What was happening between them was too important to be trifled with; he'd planned to go slowly and get it right.

But Heather had a way of making him forget his intentions. Cradling her face in his palms, he bent his head to nibble gently on her lower lip, his body catching fire as she responded with undisguised eagerness, her arms twining around his neck. As he laced his fingers through her hair and pressed his other palm on the base of her spine so she would feel the hardness and pulsating energy she'd aroused in him, Josh deepened the kiss, his tongue parting her lips and sampling her sweet nectar with rhythmic, deep thrusts.

Clinging to Josh, sifting her fingers through the silky hair at the nape of his neck, instinctively moving her hips against his, Heather lost all awareness of everything but this strong, beautiful man who held her in his arms.

Josh pushed his self-control right to the limit as he moved his hand from Heather's back to smooth his palm over her cheek, then her throat, then slowly, slowly downward, slipping under her blazer so that only the fragile cotton of her blouse protected her skin from his searing touch. Still enjoying the bounty of her mouth, he caressed the upper slope of one breast with his fingertips, making feathery circles that arced closer and closer to her hardening nipple until at last he filled his hand with the soft, generous breast, then repeated his ministrations on the other.

As he felt himself edging toward the brink, he knew he had to stop before it became impossible. And he did have to stop, if only to prove to himself that the Josh Campbell he was trying to become wouldn't settle for fleeting pleasure. Not with this woman.

Reluctantly releasing her mouth, Josh wrapped his arms around Heather and cuddled her as if she were fragile, feeling her heart throbbing in unison with his.

When he'd restored himself to some semblance of calm, and Heather's labored breathing had returned almost to normal, Josh crooked his index finger under her chin to tilt her face up toward him. "I'd better be on my way, Muffin. Otherwise, you're liable to ask me in to look at your etchings, and I'm liable to accept, and we're more than liable to do something we're not ready for." With a chaste kiss to Heather's forehead, Josh grasped her shoulders and gently pushed himself away from her, then hurried out of the house, looking back from the footpath only once. "Lock your door," he said with a fierce look before turning to stride toward his car.

Heather shut the door behind him, started into the house, then stopped and returned to the entryway, her movements automatic.

She didn't know whether to be touched by Josh's gentlemanliness or insulted by his abrupt departure. The one thing she was certain of was that she was disappointed. "They sure aren't making Viking raiders the way they used to," she muttered, turning the heavy key in the lock.

Glancing at herself in the oval, gilt-framed hallway mirror, she thrust out her full, kiss-swollen lower lip in a slight pout. "Or maybe," she said with a deep sigh, "he's not too keen on this year's crop of Saxon maidens."

Josh was working on the engine of a 1953 Mercedes when Maharg stalked purposefully into the garage and pounded his stick on the floor. "Campbell! Where's Heather?"

"At the moment she's at her office," Josh answered without looking up. The weekend of the clan gathering had arrived, and Maharg had a bad case of what Mrs. Dalrymple good-naturedly called his "crotcheties." "But I'll be picking her up in a couple of hours and get her here well before your visitors arrive," Josh went on pleasantly.

Maharg peered under the car's hood to watch what Josh was doing. "Right. Well, that's fine, but I still don't understand how those Yanks will find their way."

Suppressing a sigh, Josh willed himself to be as patient with Maharg as Heather always was. But the man's habit of asking questions and then not listening to the answers could be frustrating. "As Heather has explained," Josh said with mild reproach, "one of her tour guides will be at the airport to meet the plane and put your people on a bus; even the driver has been checked out to be sure he knows where this place is. Have faith in *Dreamweavers*, Maharg. Heather and her staff know what they're doing."

"I hope so," Maharg grumbled. "This blasted clan gathering is going to be the death of me, that's what it is." He moved closer to watch what Josh was doing to the Mercedes.

Josh smiled. "More like the life of you, my friend. You can't wait for the festivities to begin."

With twinkling eyes and a suppressed grin, Maharg changed the subject. "What's going on under this poor old lady's bonnet, Campbell? Are you going to be able to get her back on the road?"

Straightening up, Josh wiped his hands on a rag and motioned to Maharg to stand back while he shut the car's hood. "Let's give her a try," he said with a smile. Sliding behind the wheel, he gave Maharg a confident wink, and a moment later the Mercedes roared to life.

"You're a miracle worker, lad. A miracle worker." Maharg sighed happily. "Och, it's good to hear the lady purring again."

"It's always good to hear ladies purring," Josh said, switching off the ignition.

Maharg chuckled, but gave Josh one of his best glowers. "I trust you're not hearing any purrs but Heather's these days. I wouldn't like to see the lass hurt, Campbell. You two have been seeing a great deal of each other for these past weeks."

Josh got out of the car and shut the door, musing that no one could imagine how much self-control he'd been exerting to be sure Heather wasn't hurt. It had been his idea to make sure they always went out with others, whether Maggie and Donald, Annie and Rob, or the high-spirited members of the *Dreamweavers* tour guide staff. He hadn't dared to be alone with Heather for more than their good night kisses, and even those had been difficult to keep tame. "You're pretty fond of Heather," he said to Maharg.

"Aye, and who wouldn't be? You know, you'd do well to put your brand on her while you have the chance."

Josh laughed more heartily than the comment deserved. "Put my brand on her? You sound more like a Texas redneck than a Scottish laird."

"There's not as much difference between the two as you might think, lad. And chortle if you will, but a lass like Heather Sinclair doesn't come along every day, and the man who lets her pass by is making the mistake of his life."

"Speaking of Texas rednecks," Josh said, not ready for this turn in the conversation, "I might have a buyer for the Daimler."

"A Texan?" Maharg asked, instantly diverted from his matchmaking efforts.

"No, just a guy in Florida who's as rich as a Texan, according to a buddy of mine there who's another classic-car buff," Josh answered with a grin. "Should I go ahead and try to make the sale?"

Maharg took off his porkpie hat, raked his fingers through his white hair, then clamped the hat back on. "You mean, am I having second thoughts?" He shook his head. "You know, my mother always talked about how she wanted to retire to Florida, or at least winter in Palm Beach. But somehow, she never got there. She'd be happy to know her favorite car managed to do it. No, Campbell, I'll not change my mind. If you can find buyers for all but the Bentley—that one I'll keep— then do it. And I have friends with old buggies that aren't being so much as glanced at from one year to the next. You've the beginnings of a thriving import-export business on your hands if you want it, lad. And the cars are only the beginning. Wait until I start showing you the furniture and paintings and such, just gathering dust in storerooms around this countryside." As Josh locked up the garage, Maharg's attention returned to his clan gathering. "What about you, Campbell? Will you lose your nerve about tonight?"

"Lose my nerve? A Campbell?" Josh said with mock incredulity.

"You've not told Heather what we're up to, have you?"

"Not a word."

"Good," Maharg said, his whole face alight with anticipation. "I can't wait to see her expression when the proper moment comes."

Josh laughed again, but he wasn't as eager as Maharg. He just hoped Heather was as good a sport as she seemed.

Heather checked her watch as she reached for the phone on her desk. It was almost time for Josh to pick her up to take her to Maharg's for the long-awaited weekend, and she had only one very pleasant chore to do before going: She had to call Annie MacLean with the news that the vacation Annie and Rob wanted to take in the south of France was well within their budget after all.

"Hi," she said when Annie answered. "I talked to Lisa. It happens that she and Pete are planning a trip to the States, so their villa will be empty for two weeks and they'd love someone to be there to house-sit. The place is yours if you want it."

Annie gasped. "But your sister doesn't even know us!"

"My sister trusts my judgment," Heather said. "I told her you'd water the plants and keep Pete's Steinway polished, and she said she'd leave the key for you at her office. All we have to do is coordinate dates and times."

"Heather, I didna expect anythin' like this," Annie muttered, her accent thickening, a sure sign of excitement.

"Good. Then it's a surprise, and I love surprises. So just accept graciously and dream about the Riviera."

"Dream?" Annie said, an odd catch in her voice.

Heather knew her neighbor too well. "Annie, have you been seeing me slung like a sack of oats over Josh's shoulder again?"

"No, nothin' like that," Annie said hesitantly.

Heather scowled at the telephone. "You're making me nervous. Tell me everything, Annie. It couldn't be worse than what I'll imagine if you don't."

"It probably means nothing," Annie said, adding in a rush of words. "My dreams dinna always come true, you know. And it was just a fleetin' scene: Josh, wearin' a kilt for some reason, a Campbell tartan, lyin' stone-cold still on the grass, his eyes shut, and you beside him, cryin' as if your very heart was broken."

The memory she'd been suppressing for weeks was triggered again in Heather's consciousness; she couldn't quite capture it, and didn't want to. "What was I wearing? A homespun gown?" she asked, determined to treat the whole thing as a joke.

"I believe you were in faded blue denim," Annie answered. "Yes, that's what it was. Jeans and a chambray shirt."

Heather smiled, undeniably relieved. "The only jeans I have are too new to be faded. I don't even own a chambray shirt, and I certainly wouldn't be likely to wear such a casual outfit if Josh were in a kilt—in the improbable event that he'd be decked out in such regalia. I don't think we need to worry about this dream too much."

Annie gave another sigh. "You're right. And 'tis good I talked to you, because I have to admit I was bothered by that one. I'm much happier to watch my first dream about Josh comin' true."

"Don't be too sure," Heather said hastily. "Josh hasn't thrown me over his shoulder yet to carry me off to unknown destinations."

"But now you're no' so certain you'd mind if he did, lass. You're a wee bit wishin' he'd get 'round to it."

Heather felt a flush rising over her throat and face. Annie was right on the mark; Josh was playing the gentleman far beyond the point of reason, and his good night kisses at the door were enough to drive any healthy female to distraction. "As I suggested earlier, Annie," Heather said with excessive perkiness, "go and dream of the Riviera."

Annie laughed. "And you be sure to have a grand

time at Sir Alasdair's. You're stayin' for the whole weekend?"

"Until late Sunday afternoon," Heather answered. She looked up as Jessie Cameron opened her door, the receptionist's black look heralding Josh's arrival. "I have to go, Annie," Heather said hastily, unable to contain her eagerness. "I'll tell you all about the gathering when I see you. 'Bye."

"Mr. *Campbell* is here," Jessie intoned.

Heather stood, grabbed her shoulder bag and small suitcase from the old-fashioned wardrobe where she'd stashed them earlier, smoothed down the straight skirt of her coral linen dress, and smiled with feigned innocence. "Josh tells me he's going to capture you for at least one dance at the ball tonight, Jessie."

Jessie's harrumph, Heather thought, lacked conviction.

"Hi, Muffin," Josh said, automatically reaching for Heather's suitcase.

Heather smiled. "Hi," she said softly. In that moment, her whole being suddenly infused with new vibrance just because of Josh's presence, Heather made up her mind. If the Viking raider wouldn't come to the Saxon maiden . . .

Ten

Following Josh along the corridor of the old wing of Maharg's house, Heather said in a hushed voice, "If I don't spot a ghost here, I'll give up hope of ever seeing one."

"Why are you whispering?" Josh asked in a stage whisper of his own.

Heather giggled. "I don't know. I suppose the exposed timbers and vaulted ceilings give me the same feeling I get in ancient cathedrals. Or maybe it's the family portraits lining these red-brocade walls. I'm sure Maharg's ancestors will shush me if I don't show the proper reverence."

Smiling absently, Josh stopped in front of an ornately carved oak door and pushed it open.

Heather grinned as the door actually creaked. "I'm going to love this room," she said, still unable to speak in a normal voice, as if afraid of disturbing the castle's invisible denizens.

"Mrs. Dalrymple has been wringing her hands all week," Josh said as Heather preceded him into the bedroom. "The poor woman just can't understand why you asked to be put here. She keeps fussing about how there's a much nicer room you could have had in the newer part of the house, with pretty wallpaper and a lovely pink comforter on the bed and furniture that was bought in this very century."

Heather giggled at Josh's affectionate mimicry, her approving glance taking in the stone fireplace, the heavy furnishings and draperies, the rich velvets and damasks of a room that could have been the set of a Gothic horror movie. "Ghosts absolutely have to wander through this wing," she murmured.

"And the idea of confronting a spirit holds no fear whatsoever for you?" Josh asked with a grin, placing her overnight bag on a heavy, dark bureau.

"None whatsoever," Heather insisted as she sat on the edge of the bed and tested it with a couple of bounces.

"Not even malevolent ones? What if you get a visit from the murderous mistress?"

"Och, I can handle the likes of that one," Heather answered, refusing to let Josh scare her.

"Well, if she gets too nasty, my room's right down the hall," he said casually.

Heather stared at him. "Down the hall? Are there other guests in this wing?"

"Just the two of us, Muffin. And don't worry about my motives or about what anyone's going to think of this arrangement. There was just no way Maharg or Mrs. Dalrymple or I would let you stay in this gloomy old section of the house all by yourself."

Heather tilted her head to one side, suppressing a smile of surprise and secret pleasure. "It's not *your* motives I'm thinkin' about," she murmured.

It was Josh's turn to stare. Then, clearing his

throat, he started backing out of the room. "I have a lot to do before tonight," he said with uncharacteristic edginess. "For one thing, I promised Mrs. Dalrymple I'd keep Maharg out of her hair. And Finch needs—" Abruptly stopping, Josh laughed at himself. "I'll meet you at the entrance to the dining room just before dinner, okay?"

With a quizzical smile, Heather nodded. She'd never seen Josh so off balance.

Heather stood in the foyer just outside the entrance to the dining room, waiting for Josh and greeting Maharg's guests, her floor-length white silk dress a pristine background for the MacGregor tartan shawl she'd looped over one hip and draped over her shoulder, then fastened with a pewter pin bearing the coat of arms of her mother's once-outlawed clan.

She surveyed the scene with deep satisfaction. Everything was perfect, from the soft lighting provided by the polished crystal chandeliers, to the gleaming parquet floors, to the beautifully appointed table in the huge dining room. The guests already milling about were dressed formally, the women elegant in cocktail dresses or traditional white gowns with tartan shawls, the men resplendent in dinner jackets or kilts.

Maharg had received them with the aplomb of royalty, showing a smoothly charming side to his gruff character that amazed and delighted Heather. He was in his element. And he'd already told her he was looking forward to having his home become a regular *Dreamweavers* feature.

Her only disappointment was that Josh hadn't come down from his room yet. Eager to see how handsome he would look in a tux, looking forward to being his chosen lady for the ball, she'd been as excited as a teenager all day. But she was beginning to wonder if he'd forgotten about being her escort. Of course, he'd known she would be busy at the start of the evening, getting acquainted with Maharg's guests—her clients—but it was nearly time for dinner and he hadn't arrived to claim her.

Maharg moved to stand beside Heather as she glanced toward the great staircase that led to the old wing of the house. "You're watching for your Lochinvar, are you? Well, have no fear. He'll be along any minute now—unless he's lost his nerve, which I doubt."

Heather frowned. "Lost his nerve? You mean because he's a Campbell? Josh knew he might face some heavy teasing this weekend, but he accepted your invitation anyway. Why would he lose his nerve at the last minute?"

As Maharg moved away, his wicked chuckle warned Heather that he was up to something. He'd been beaming with self-satisfaction ever since she and Josh had started seeing each other. Heaven knew what he was planning now.

A moment later, she found out what it was, and her heart leapt into her throat.

Like a hero conjured up from her own romantic imagination, Josh stood at the top of the stairs, his lips curved in a smile as devilish as Maharg's, his magnificent body clad in the full regalia of a Campbell tartan kilt.

Heather's knees threatened to give out. Hearing someone in the room give a surprised laugh and, recognizing Josh's plaid, whisper that a Campbell was in their midst, Heather realized what a bold move Josh had made. And she knew instantly that Maharg had been in on the mischief.

Shaken by the intense eroticism of her reaction to Josh but filled with admiration for him, Heather stared for a long moment, then began applauding slowly and deliberately. Maharg joined her, then several other people, amusement and appreciation of Josh's sheer bravado spreading throughout the crowd. Jessie Cameron's hands remained at her sides, but even she couldn't suppress a tiny smile.

Josh walked toward Heather and bowed deeply when he reached her, offering her his arm, golden flames flickering in his eyes as his gaze swept over her. "Do you have any idea how lovely you are?" he added in a low, caressing voice that sent tingles through her.

"I could stand to be told, Campbell," she said softly, taking his arm.

"How many hours do we have?" he murmured as he led her to the table.

The meal was a triumph, the host a delight, the guests obviously thrilled to be entertained in what they rightly considered their ancestral seat.

The weekend was off to a fine start.

When the company retired to the ballroom for dancing late in the evening, Heather wondered how Josh would manage. It was doubtful that his male-oriented background had included lessons in ballroom dancing, much less the traditional selections the fiddler and the small orchestra were slated to play.

But she quickly discovered how wrong she was as Josh whirled her in a masterful waltz, his steps light and sure, his hand guiding her with a firmness that made him easy to follow.

Throughout the evening, he displayed his perfect schottische, spirited reel, and faultless quadrille. "All right, confess," Heather said, grinning up at him during another waltz, just after he'd led a beaming Jessie Cameron through a Gay Gordon. "You didn't learn those steps on a dock in Florida or on an oil rig in the Shetlands."

"Maybe I remember them from a past life," Josh teased, holding Heather closer than was proper, loving the way her every move seemed almost uncannily attuned to his lead.

"The truth," Heather insisted.

"Mrs. Dalrymple taught me," he admitted. "She's a very patient lady." He didn't bother to add how foolish he'd felt when he'd asked the housekeeper to coach him, or how hard it had been to admit that his upbringing had left gaps in his command of certain social graces.

Deeply touched that Josh would go so far to please her—and she had no doubt whatsoever that pleasing her had been his motive—Heather nestled still closer to him, her lips next to his ear. "You're the loveliest man there ever was," she murmured.

Excited by the warmth of Heather's breath against his skin, Josh spoke in a husky voice. "Let's just say I'm doing my best to live up to the image you seem to have of me. But I warn you," he added with an almost shy laugh, "I've a long way to go."

Heather tipped back her head to favor him with a glower that would have done Maharg proud. "Do this lass a wee favor, Campbell," she said with her best Scottish burr. "The next time you feel the urge to issue me a warnin' about somethin' or other, stop and remember that there's a better use for those sweet, manly lips o' yours."

Laughing, Josh whirled her through the French doors that opened out into the terrace, danced her toward a giant oak in the garden, and gently pinioned her against the trunk, his hands on either side of her shoulders. "As it happens, lass," he said with a creditable accent of his own, "I seem to be feelin' another warnin' comin' on."

Heather twined her arms around his neck and parted her lips just in time to give his warm, firm, delicious mouth something better to do.

Just as Heather had expected, Josh said good night to her at her bedroom door. She wanted to shake him, or at least mention that there was such a thing as carrying gallantry too far. But no matter, she thought. She had her own plans for how the night would end.

Stripping to the buff, she let the cool, dewy breeze caress her naked body before she slid into her nightgown, a lightweight, sleeveless confection in sheer white cotton, its low, square-neck bodice sewn into countless tiny pleats that were released just under her breasts to let the skirt fall softly to a lace-trimmed hem that grazed her ankles.

Heather surveyed herself in a freestanding, mahogany-framed mirror. She remembered the day she'd bought the nightgown several months before in a sinfully luxurious shop in London. It had seemed a ridiculous splurge, but for some reason she'd felt she just had to have the gown. And with the same kind of compulsion, she'd brought it along for the weekend at Maharg's.

Smiling, she looked herself in the eye and admitted that buying the nightgown might have been a mad impulse, but packing it had been less than innocent in intent. Outright seduction might not have been on her mind, and she hadn't been planning wickedness when she'd asked for a room in the old-castle section of the house—she hadn't known Josh would be placed in the same wing—but things did seem to be working out rather nicely.

A crazy plan she'd begun to hatch earlier in the evening to lure Josh into her sensual web began to seem plausible in the secret, quiet dark of the night.

Heather took her hair down from its topknot and ran a brush through her curls, then refreshed her fragrance with a spritz of floral-and-musk cologne. Ready to assume the unfamiliar role of seductress, she took several deep breaths and let them out very slowly, then gave herself a mental push.

Her bedroom door creaked when she opened it. Heather smiled. The eerie sound was perfect.

In her bare feet, she moved silently along the hallway to Josh's room and knocked quietly on his door.

Josh opened it. He looked startled.

"Ghosts," Heather whispered, her heart beginning to pound as she realized that Josh was either naked or nearly so under his black cotton kimono.

Josh gave her a quizzical smile. "Ghosts?"

Heather nodded. "In my room."

"I thought you weren't afraid of them," Josh said, his voice low and vibrating with excitement, the desire that had been held hostage too firmly and for too long sensing release.

"I'm not afraid of them," Heather said with a lift of her chin. "But I've just learned from a wee fairy sittin' outside my window that the jealous madwoman who haunts these halls hates men with a passion—especially braw, bonny lads with pale hair and the strength of Eric the Red and Leif the

Lucky put together. So when she started floatin' around my chamber, obviously doin' her rounds, I decided I'd better hurry along here to protect you."

Reaching out to take Heather's hand and gently draw her into his room, Josh was surprised to find how cold she was. She was shivering a little. He closed the heavy door behind her, then took both her hands between his palms to warm them.

Suddenly, looking at Heather, Josh felt the impact of her loveliness as never before. Her hair, loose for the first time since the day she'd appeared on the country road near Alva Glen, was like an aura of firelight framing her clear, strong features. Her skin was almost translucent, flagged at her high cheekbones with the same soft pink that tinted her full, parted lips. Her eyes were dark with promise as she gazed up at him, glints of excitement and mischief and anxiety playing in their depths like sprites in a secret forest.

And as Heather stood in a swath of light shed by his night-table lamp, her womanly curves clearly silhouetted and belying the Victorian innocence of her white nightgown, Josh knew that the spell of enchantment she had cast over him would last forever. "How can you protect me from ghosts, Heather?" he asked, barely able to speak, hardly able to breathe.

She smiled hesitantly. "By loving you," she said softly. "No ghost can harm a person who's protected by the power of love."

Releasing Heather's hands, Josh lifted her in his arms and carried her to the bed, finally letting his overflowing emotions take control. "Then we're both safe from poltergeists," he murmured as he gently placed Heather on the thick comforter and stretched out beside and half over her, resting his weight on his forearms as he tenderly cradled her. "Because between us," he added, brushing his lips over her face in a shower of soft kisses, "we're generating enough love to ease any restless spirit."

Heather's eyes filled with sudden tears. "You don't have to . . . I didn't say I love you so I could hear it, Josh. There's no price tag. I'm not bartering for—"

Josh touched his lips to hers to quiet her, then raised his head and smiled. "I know, Heather. You don't barter. You just give. That's part of why . . ." He paused. He'd always thought of himself as a risk-taker, a reasonably brave man. Yet it was requiring all his courage to undo the last padlocks on his emotions. But after only a moment, he knew he had no lingering doubts. "It's part of why I love you, Heather. And I do love you. I didn't know I had the capacity, but you've shown me that I have. And the best part is that we've hardly begun. Can you imagine what's ahead for us?"

As Heather's tears spilled over, Josh kissed them away, then grazed his lips over her temple to her cheek, her throat, the tip of her chin, finally capturing her lips to toy with them. Heather clasped her hands behind his head and silently but eloquently demanded the kind of deep, searing kiss they both wanted so desperately.

Dizzy with pleasure, Heather sifted Josh's hair through her fingers, then stroked the corded nape of his neck, slipping her hands under his robe as her palms sought out the smooth warmth of his back and shoulders. Each touch made her crave more, and soon she instinctively pushed at his robe, her fingers feathering over his collarbone and down onto the broad expanse of his chest. Marveling at the rigid hardness of his breastbone, the stiffening of his flat nipples, the silkiness of the coils of chest hair, she found herself moving her body against him in an unmistakable signal of urgent need.

Already wild with unappeased hunger, Josh wasn't sure he could regain enough control to give Heather all the pleasure he wanted her to have. Loving her made him determined to be patient, yet paradoxically made patience almost impossible. As if he were an inexperienced boy, his fingers shook and fumbled a little when they went to the tiny buttons at the front of her gown. "Stop," he whispered as Heather's hands roved over his body, inflaming him until he was dangerously close to an explosion.

Heather froze. What had she done wrong?

But Josh smiled reassuringly, though he was struggling to catch his breath. "Wait, love," he urged raggedly. "I want you too much, Heather, and we need to take time—"

"No!" Heather cried with sheer joy and relief to know that she hadn't done anything wrong, that Josh did want her as much as she wanted him. "You can take all the time you like later," she urged. "Right now, just take me. Please, Josh," she said more gently. "Just take me."

Josh gazed down at Heather for a long moment, then simply surrendered. And in that moment, as he let go of every vestige of his struggle to control his feelings, his shakiness was gone. He helped Heather rid him of his robe, then easily undid each tiny button of her nightgown, revealing her glorious femininity inch by lovely inch. A moment later, as the gown floated to the floor, he stroked his fingers and palms over her soft, cool skin, exploring every rise and hollow of her body, every subtle change in texture, every nuance of her responses. He kissed her mouth with new gentleness, then drew the tip of his tongue downward, following a pulsating pathway along her throat, then farther, over the slope of each of her full breasts, finally swirling his tongue around the velvety pink aureole, taking the engorged nipple between his lips and gently suckling.

At first Heather was mesmerized, floating on a wave of erotic delight, then she became increasingly excited, until she was gasping with shock after shock of ecstasy. Josh's hands and mouth discovered secrets of pleasuring Heather even she hadn't known about: a certain way of touching his tongue to the inside of her elbow, to a sensitive hollow of her shoulder, to the underside of her breast; a feathering of his fingers over her stomach, over the insides of her thighs; and an unerring knowledge of the things he could do to a special spot that turned her universe into a maelstrom of bursting lights and color and unbearable joy.

When at last Josh moved over her, parting her thighs and poising himself at the entrance to the essence of her femininity, Heather's eyes were glazed, as if she were drugged.

"I love you," Josh whispered. "I love you, Heather Sinclair. And I take back every warning I ever gave you, because the Josh Campbell I was talking about doesn't exist anymore." He smiled with infinite tenderness. "You sprinkled some kind of magic dust on him and transformed him into a new person."

Heather smiled, returned his words of love on a languid sigh, then closed her eyes as she opened herself to Josh's rigid heat, her own warmth closing around him as they began to move in a joined rhythm that was as easy and natural to them as the mere act of existing.

Josh was amazed by the serenity that settled over him, the patience of his body, the wholeness of his spirit. It was as if he'd waited forever to become part of Heather, his inner being fragmented until he'd found her, and now he could make a gradual climb toward the inevitable peak, not needing to rush the journey.

But his movements—or perhaps Heather's movements—began to quicken. His love for Heather gathered into a volatile force, compressing into a tight coil of pure energy.

As Josh's arms tightened around her and he thrust more and more deeply into her, Heather found her body rising to meet him as if to engulf him, to receive eagerly whatever he could give her. Vaguely, she remembered fearing Josh's extravagant maleness. Not now. Now his masculine power was part of the gift he gave her, as her own kind of strength was what she could offer him.

Something ignited inside her at the moment of that realization. Josh's body tightened as a deep groan was torn from his throat, and he held her as she'd never dreamed she would be held.

Clinging to him, whispering his name and her words of love over and over, Heather floated for what seemed like a small eternity among shooting stars and whirling suns, where there was no reality except the sweet ecstasy of loving Josh.

And that reality was the only one she needed.

Eleven

The morning sun was pouring light and warmth through the small arched window in Josh's room, the shadows of the leaded panes creating intricate designs on the tapestry carpet, when Heather's eyelids flew open.

Bolting upright, she stared at the crisscross patterns but didn't see them, her heart pounding out of control.

Josh stirred, then opened his eyes and sat up as he saw the rigidity of Heather's back, the trembling of her body. He hoped she wasn't having morning-after regrets, though he didn't see how she could. Not after the night of love they'd shared. "What is it, Heather?" he asked.

She turned to stare at him. "You wore a kilt."

Josh's smile was puzzled. "It took you until now to notice?"

"But I wasn't wearing jeans and a chambray shirt," Heather said, chewing on her lip. "So maybe it's all right."

Putting his arms around Heather, Josh drew her close and lay back on the pillows, cuddling her. "Honey, did you have a bad dream?" he asked gently.

"No, Annie did," Heather blurted out. "But it's okay, because nothing happened. And her first dream about you didn't come true. Not exactly, anyway."

"Annie's *first* dream about me?" Thoroughly confused, Josh put the tip of his index finger under Heather's chin and lifted it up. "Start from the beginning, Muffin. And try not to make too many detours."

In halting phrases, Heather related what Annie had told her the day before, and then, with some embarrassment, went on with the details of Annie's original vision of Josh.

He laughed quietly, rather enjoying the mental image. "So I threw you over my shoulder like a sack of oats, did I? Carried you off to some secret lair without so much as a by-your-leave?"

"Never mind that," Heather said, blushing furiously. "What bothered me was Annie's latest dream. How could I have put it out of my mind so completely that I didn't think of it even when you showed up in a kilt?"

"Perhaps some common sense is starting to replace the foolish mysticism you dabble in?" Josh suggested mildly, his hand straying to Heather's smoothly rounded shoulders, then her full, soft breasts as he began thinking about a far more intriguing pursuit than discussing Annie's dream.

"Perhaps," Heather said with a sigh. Instantly aroused, she surrendered once again to pure, sweet sensation. There was no reason to worry, she told herself before her thinking processes went on hold. "You haven't treated me anything like a sack of oats, you haven't carted me off to unknown places, and even though you did wear your kilt last night, nothing dreadful happened. So everything's just fine." She sighed again as Josh's knowing touch sent delicious tingles of delight through her whole body. "Just fine," she whispered, becoming aware that Josh's magnificent physique was hers to enjoy and explore in the clear light of morning.

Deciding that the time wasn't right to tell Heather that he planned to wear his kilt for the Highland Games portion of Maharg's weekend, Josh put Annie's odd dream out of his mind and concentrated on expanding the repertoire of pleasures he and Heather could discover together.

Heather blanched when she saw Josh appear on the area of the estate's grounds that had been set aside for the games, a long field straight back from the garden at the rear of the house. "You're wearing your kilt again!" she said accusingly.

"Of course," Josh answered with a grin. "If I'm going to toss a caber among these Graham and Cameron and MacDonald athletes Maharg invited to put on a good show for the visitors, I have to wear my clan colors."

"You're what?" Heather asked, shocked. "You're entering the caber toss? Good grief, throwing a log the size of a telephone pole takes practice!"

"Don't worry, Muffin. Didn't I mention to you once that after Maggie had put me through her physiotherapist's tortures, she turned me over to Donald for a bit of special training?"

"Well, yes," Heather said with a frown. "You did mention something. But caber tossing?"

Josh laughed. "Donald figured I couldn't do anything better to build myself up than by mastering a Highlander's tests of strength. I don't expect to make much of a showing against the ringers

Maharg has brought in, but it'll be fun just to take part."

Heather said nothing more about the matter, knowing Josh well enough to realize that neither her nervous sixth sense nor Annie's dream would satisfy him as reason enough to back out of the contest, or even to change out of his kilt.

She tried to enjoy the afternoon, wandering around with Josh to watch a lively shinty match, then a first-rate troupe of Highland dancers and a small pipe band.

Beginning to relax, Heather was with Josh at the refreshment area just outside the garden, admiring a trio of typical Scottish children, all rosy-cheeked and big-eyed and fair-haired, their excited chatter all the more appealing for their thick accents, when Josh handed her the tall paper cup of orange soda she'd asked for.

"What a great day," Josh said, taking a long pull of the beer he'd opted for. "You know, Heather, you were right to talk Maharg into inviting some local guests along with their kids to mingle with the visitors. I've overheard several of your tour people mention how much they like the country-village atmosphere, and Maharg's in his glory playing the laird number to the hilt—though he did tell me that the shinty's pretty tame, what with the players being too sober and overly civilized."

Heather laughed and raised her drink to her lips just as a young woman from the tour group, walking with long, loping strides toward the refreshment stand, turned to say something to her companion, caught her toe in a loose clump of earth, and, starting to lose her balance, instinctively flailed her arms just enough to hit Heather's cup, dumping the orange soda all the way down Heather's front.

"Oh my gosh, I'm so sorry!" the horrified blonde cried, trying to wipe away the mess and succeeding only in making it worse. "I've ruined your outfit!" she said, clearly stricken. "Come into the house right away. We'll go to my room so you can change while I rinse these things out. I have some jeans and a shirt you can borrow—"

"No!" Heather said hastily, her throat suddenly constricted with fear. She managed a smile. "I mean, it's no problem. I brought along an extra outfit just in case." Even if she hadn't, she thought, she would spend the rest of the afternoon naked before she would help Annie's dream come true by wearing jeans. She didn't even want to know whether the shirt being offered was chambray. She turned to Josh. "I'll run along and change and get back in time to watch your caber-tossing prowess," she said, adding quietly, "if you really must do it."

Josh himself was slightly spooked by the way the elements of Annie's dream seemed to be adding up. But he refused to give in to superstition. "I really must," he said quietly, then leaned forward and gave her a gentle kiss on the cheek. "I'll be fine, honey. If you start letting this kind of tomfoolery rule your life, you're in real trouble."

She nodded, agreeing. And yet . . .

By the time she'd returned, wearing white slacks and a bright green T-shirt, the caber toss was in progress. She stood behind the makeshift rope barrier and watched a burly Scotsman run with the trunk of a young tree in his hands, then vault it into the air so it flipped end over end before finally landing. Heather's hands grew damp with perspiration.

When Josh's turn came, her nerves were frayed to the limit. She couldn't talk herself out of her sick dread, and just as Josh was about to make his toss, she was struck by a feeling of terror that she knew was rooted in something much deeper and more ominous than Annie's strange dream—something she couldn't identify, nagging at the edge of her consciousness, just as it had from the first day she'd known Josh.

Suddenly aware that Josh was making his running start, Heather watched nervously but proudly as he gave the log a push-off with his strong, muscular arms. It sailed high, then tumbled end over end, at last landing a respectable distance away, in a line as straight and true as any Scot could hope for.

Heather realized that she'd been expecting something terrible to happen, and it hadn't. People were clapping for Josh as he left the field.

Breathing freely for the first time in a while, Heather almost laughed aloud with relief, telling herself how silly she'd been to get worked up about such nonsense.

When Josh rejoined her in the spectator area, she congratulated him for an excellent showing and said nothing about her ridiculous fears.

Jessie Cameron, proudly holding her three-year-old granddaughter, moved to stand beside Josh and give him a shy smile. "You did well, lad."

He beamed at her. "Why thank you, Jessie."

She nodded, then gave a sniff. "For a Campbell," she added, her smile turning mischievous as she winked at him.

"Put me down, Nana?" her grandchild asked.

"Och, all right, Katie," Jessie replied, shaking her head when the little girl immediately started squirming impatiently. "But don't be such a wee worm, lass!"

At the very moment that the next contestant

started his run with the caber, Katie wriggled out of Jessie's grasp and broke free, ducking down to crawl with lightning speed under the rope barrier and tear out onto the field while the log headed directly toward her.

"Katie!" her grandmother screamed.

Josh was over the rope in an instant and dashing after the little girl.

Everything seemed to switch to slow motion for Heather. She saw the log making an arc against the clear blue of the sky, curving down toward Katie. She saw Josh grab the child by the shoulders, lift her, pivot on his heel, and sweep her out of the path of the massive, lumbering projectile. And she saw the tree trunk catch him on the side of the head as he tried in vain to duck.

Frozen, Heather looked down at her clothes as if to deny the reality of what had happened. She didn't understand. She wasn't wearing denims and a chambray shirt. How could Annie's dream have come true? "Josh," she whispered. "No, Josh. Please, please, no."

All at once, with perfect clarity, she remembered. She'd known all along that she mustn't love Josh. She'd been warned. Years and years before, it had been predicted what would happen to this man if she let herself love him.

Jessie was holding her grandchild to her side while kneeling beside Josh, wiping blood from his head with a handkerchief.

Heather had no recollection of going to him, but she was kneeling over him as well, tears rolling down her cheeks. If he died, she thought, it would be her fault, because she'd known but had blocked out the truth she hadn't wanted to face, even after the warnings of Annie's dream. He'd survived an oil-rig explosion only to walk into the trap of her love. "Josh," she whispered, weeping inconsolably. "Josh, I shouldn't have let this happen. Please, please don't die. I'll do anything to keep you safe. I'll never see you again if that's what it takes. Just don't die, Josh."

"He's not goin' to die, lass," Jessie said in her no-nonsense way. "He's been grazed a bit, that's all."

Heather didn't believe her. Josh wasn't stirring. She wasn't sure he was breathing. She stroked his hair back from his forehead, her eyes swimming with tears. "Josh, I'm so sorry. Oh please, be all right."

"What's this?" she heard.

"Och, Sir Alisdair," Jessie answered, "the caber nicked Josh on the head when he was savin' my naughty Katie's skin, and Heather thinks he's wingin' his way to heaven, the whole thing for some unknown reason bein' her fault, and . . . and . . . Why, here's the lad now. Y'see, Heather, Josh is comin' to."

Heather blinked rapidly, trying to clear her eyes. "Josh?" she asked in a tiny, fearful voice.

To her intense joy, he moved his head from side to side, then tried to sit up. "Is the little girl all right?" he asked immediately.

Maharg pounded his walking stick against the ground. "Now, there's a lad," he said with as much pride as if Josh were his son.

"You saved my daughter's wee bairn," Jessie said. "You're a hero, that's what you are. A good man."

Josh grinned weakly and sank back to the ground. "For a Campbell," he murmured, reaching for Heather's hand.

• • •

Josh slammed down the telephone receiver, stalked out of his apartment to his car, and drove through the heavy evening traffic to Heather's place.

He'd had a week of being avoided, put off, and ignored. It was enough.

Heather's withdrawal from him had been sudden but not the least bit puzzling. "Damn fool superstitions," he muttered as he crossed the Firth of Forth bridge. He couldn't believe that Heather would allow such nonsense to spoil their happiness just when everything could be so perfect for them.

Annie was leaving Heather's house when Josh pulled into the parking area at the end of the street. "Is she home?" he asked as he got out of the car.

"Aye," Annie said. "But she won't tell me what's troublin' her. I'm wishin' I'd never mentioned that dream."

"It's not your fault, Annie," Josh said. "There's more to Heather's behavior than your dream. It came true, but with no real harm done, so there's something else going on in that head of hers. And I intend to find out what it is."

Annie gave his arm a pat as she looked toward Heather's door and rolled her eyes. "I wish you luck, Josh, but that's a very stubborn lass."

Josh nodded. "And I'm a very stubborn lad."

Though he was tempted just to walk into the house, he knew he didn't have the right, so he knocked on the door.

When Heather opened it a moment later, her eyes sparkled, and she smiled at him with such warmth, he wondered if he'd imagined the troubles of the past week.

But she sobered quickly, lowering her long lashes as if drawing a veil over the love she'd revealed.

Josh spoke in measured syllables. "I want an explanation, Heather. Now. Why the deep freeze?"

Heather stood quietly for a moment, then stepped back to let Josh in, realizing that he was in no mood to be put off any longer. Indicating the couch, she curled up in the wing chair opposite it, tucking her long, bare legs under her and pulling her flared denim skirt over them—the same skirt she'd been wearing the first time Josh had seen her. Her red shell top was the same one as well, and her hair was loose, the way it had been then and on the night they'd made love.

Josh lowered himself to the couch and kept a tight rein on the feelings his memories evoked. "Okay, Muffin. I'm listening," he said quietly.

She nodded. "I warn you, Josh, you'll think I'm being ridiculous. But here it is: When I was about nine, my parents docked the *Dreamweaver* at a tiny South Sea island where there was a huge fair going on, with all sorts of food and crafts and street entertainers."

Josh remembered that on the first day he and Heather had met, she'd started to tell him about that fair. At the time, he'd wondered vaguely why she'd stopped in the middle of the story. "And you followed Morgan everywhere," he said, to help the story along.

Heather smiled and shook her head in surprise, though she told herself that by this time she ought to know that Josh was a man who listened and remembered. It was one of the many qualities she adored in him. "That's right," she went on after a moment. "Morgan didn't know I was shadowing her. When she went to a fortune-telling booth, I hid behind a tree until she came out, and then I stole inside and spent every penny in my pocket just to have the cards read." Heather paused and chewed on her lower lip, feeling foolish. Told aloud, her story sounded even sillier than she'd feared it would.

"And what was your fortune?" Josh asked gently, curbing his impatience.

After another deep breath, Heather went on. "It seemed that I would find my soul mate in a far-off country; he'd be a very large, fair-haired man." She swallowed hard, her throat tightening as she got to the part that had frightened her into burying the prediction so deeply in her mind that she'd unwittingly constructed a safe alternative for her romantic fantasies. "The catch, however," she continued huskily, "was that loving this man would put him in mortal danger." She gave her head a little shake. "Ever since meeting you I've been plagued from time to time by a . . . an awful dread. I've tried to explain it away. I don't want to believe in such a horrible kind of predestination, but Annie's dream . . . and you were almost killed . . ." Her eyes filled with tears.

Josh got up from the couch, went over to Heather, and hunkered down in front of her, taking her hands in his. He spoke very quietly and carefully. "I'm prepared to admit that there are lots of things in this world we can't explain, Muffin. Maybe some people do have dreams that seem to pick up on future events. But that fortune-teller you're talking about just had a mean streak, not second sight. Even if she thought she really was looking into the future, those were vicious things to say to a little girl."

"But Josh, they did start to come true!"

"Big deal," he said with a teasing smile. "It's obvious that you're an American, and there you were, on a South Sea island. Naturally she said that when you grew up and fell in love, it would be in some far-off place. And she had a good chance of being right about the physical description. But did she give my name? My initials? Even my nationality? The color of my eyes? Did she talk about my scars?"

"What scars?" Heather asked, frowning.

"From the debris that hit me in the oil-rig explosion—which, by the way, I gather this seer of yours didn't read in her cards, though it was a pretty traumatic event."

Heather was shocked that she'd been so unobservant, especially considering how appreciative she was of Josh's body. "I didn't see your scars."

He grinned. "They're on my back. You didn't see much of that part of my anatomy on the one memorable night we enjoyed without being punished."

"Not punished, perhaps, but warned. I knew you'd make fun of me if I told you everything," Heather said with a pout. "It's all very fine to give rational explanations to discount everything that woman said, but what if she wasn't a fraud? Do you want to take that chance?"

Josh nodded. "As a matter of fact, I do."

"Well, I'm not sure I do," Heather said. "I couldn't forgive myself if—"

"Answer this question," Josh interrupted, his patience running out. "What was Morgan told that day? Did your sister's future unfold as it was supposed to?"

Heather looked down at her lap, not answering.

"Well?" Josh prompted.

"I have no idea what Morgan's fortune was," Heather said at last. "I didn't want her to know I'd followed her."

Suddenly Josh recoiled as if he'd been kicked. So much for taking the risk of loving, he thought with a stab of anger. He'd known better. What had made him suspend his common sense? "You haven't talked to Morgan about all this?" he asked, an edge of steel in his voice.

Unable to meet his gaze, Heather just shook her head.

Josh straightened up and looked down at her. "The real problem here isn't a fortune told to an impressionable nine-year-old who suppressed the memory of it until it grew all out of proportion. This whole thing between us, Heather—what we've felt for each other. What does it mean to you? What *can* it mean to you, when you don't even bother to talk to your sister about a pack of foolishness that's tearing us apart? Am I just another of your silly scrapes? Have you started walking down an unfamiliar road and discovered that it's the wrong one?"

Finally, Heather looked up to stare at him. "What do you mean?"

Josh met her gaze and held it for several long, tense moments. "You know, I really thought we had something. I was working out big plans for our life together, figuring out the logistics, wondering whether you would consider going back to the States, thinking we could travel here together whenever business requires it . . ." He stopped, his shoulders sagging. "What happened to the girl who was always so unflinchingly honest? The one who wasn't afraid of anything? The beautiful woman who claimed that the power of her love was invincible protection against any ghost?" With a heavy sigh, he muttered, "What a sap I've been." Then, to Heather's shocked dismay, he turned on his heel and left without another word.

Heather was rooted to the spot. She couldn't believe he'd walked out that way. Didn't he understand that it was her love for him that paralyzed her with fear? Why had he looked at her as if she were a total stranger? Why the awful pain in his eyes? The look of betrayal? How could he profess to feel so much for her, yet dismiss her so easily?

She shouldn't be surprised, she told herself. Josh was being exactly what she'd always known he was: a hard, stubborn, uncompromising male.

After a long time, she wandered into the dining room, where she'd set up her makeshift studio. Lowering herself to a straight-backed chair, she studied the photographs and sketches she'd made of Pete Cochrane, Cole Jameson, and T.J. Carriere.

Moving almost like a sleepwalker, Heather picked up a sketch pad and pencil and began making rough drawings of each of her brothers-in-law, trying to leave out certain qualities they shared, the ones that troubled her about Josh.

But she couldn't isolate their humor, their passion, or their magnetism. When their strength was left out, or their maddening stubbornness, or their occasionally domineering protectiveness, or any other facet of their vibrant personalities, the drawings became flat. Lifeless.

Minutes passed, then hours. Heather wasn't aware of time, her whole being absorbed in her efforts to create a likeness of the perfect man, one who had no daunting characteristics, whose challenges would be easy to meet, who wouldn't drive a woman to mutter, "Men!" as if it were the only epithet needed to express all that was infuriating about them.

She kept getting cardboard facades. She took the drawing pad to bed and began sketching Josh in all his moods. She was amazed by his infinite variety.

But after she'd fallen asleep, she kept seeing his

pain-filled eyes. She woke up several times, puzzled. It hadn't occurred to her that she wielded as much emotional power over Josh as he had over her.

She opened her eyes the next morning remembering the last things Josh had said to her. They were tantamount to a proposal. Or a retraction of a proposal he'd never made. She wasn't sure what.

But he'd talked about logistics, and about where they might live . . . and no one could have called him uncompromising. She would love to return to the States with him, and she knew she could work it out, yet she was touched that he hadn't taken her flexibility for granted.

All at once it hit her. What a fool she'd been! What self-deception she'd been indulging in! It wasn't Josh who was uncompromising and stubborn. *She* was! She wanted his love, but she wasn't so sure about the changes he would bring to her life. She was afraid of being overwhelmed by the sheer strength of his personality, yet hadn't *she* had to seduce *him*? Hadn't he gone so far as to learn the *quadrille*, for heaven's sake, just to please her?

And the truth about her sisters was that they'd blossomed and fulfilled themselves in countless ways since they'd teamed up with men who seemed every bit as daunting as Josh.

At last, Heather began to understand: She and her sisters wanted and needed the kind of men they'd been wise enough to fall for. And it probably took a special breed of male to appreciate and cope with the vagaries of the Sinclair women.

It was almost as an afterthought that Heather called Morgan, and when she hung up she didn't know whether to laugh or cry. She did both.

At twenty-nine, blissfully married to Cole Jameson, breathtakingly lovely, Morgan proved how phony the South Sea fortune-teller had been. "I was supposed to die a spinster, before I was twenty-five, of a disfiguring disease," she'd told Heather. Typically, Morgan had laughed off the whole thing from the start. "I wish I'd known you were being my little shadow again that day," she'd said on the phone. "I could have saved you so much needless worry. I knew that nasty old hag was a fraud when I egged her on by pretending she was right about past events. I really had her going there for a while. But Heather, Josh is right. That crazy prediction isn't what scares you about loving him. You're suffering from what Steffie and I have decided is the Sinclair Syndrome: Every one of us has come up with some kind of far-out excuse—well, maybe not quite as colorful as a fortune-teller's dumb prediction—that keeps us from facing the simple fact that we've fallen for strong men, then started getting cold feet, thinking maybe they're *too* strong. But they're not, Heather." Morgan had given her low, husky chuckle. "Men can't be too strong for the likes of us."

Heather's call to Josh wasn't as successful. He wasn't home. She tried all evening. No luck. She called Maggie and Don. No answer. She phoned Maharg. "He's leaving, lass," Maharg said. "He's flying to New York tomorrow, says he wants to put in his two shillings worth—two cents worth, I guess he put it—at some investigation into oil-rig safety. Then he's off to Florida to put his import-export company in place. Go after him, lass."

"Do you know what flight he'll be on?" Heather asked. She was taken aback; while she'd been paralyzed, Josh had swung into action. On the verge of feeling hurt that he hadn't been licking his wounds, she suddenly remembered the sketches that wouldn't work unless they were true. She tried to picture Josh moping, but had to smile. It wouldn't work. It wasn't true. And she wouldn't have him any other way.

Josh was in line at the departure lounge at the Edinburgh airport, heartsick at the thought of leaving Scotland even though he knew he would be back, if only for business reasons.

He'd hoped to hear from Heather. He couldn't believe she would let fear stifle her love. He'd been brutal with her at the end as a last-ditch attempt to shock her into seeing how her fear of the unknown was the only obstacle in the way of their happiness. But his gamble hadn't paid off.

"Boarding pass, please," a petite, uniformed woman said as Josh stepped up to the security gate.

"Wait!" he heard behind him.

He froze, closing his eyes for a moment as if to be sure he wasn't imagining things.

"Please go ahead," the security guard said with a note of impatience.

Josh stepped out of line and turned in time to catch Heather as she hurled herself against him.

"You forgot something!" she said, burying her face in the familiar, fragrant warmth of his throat.

"What did I forget?" he asked, his voice hoarse with emotion as he closed his arms about her.

She tipped back her head and laughed softly. "Your sack of oats, Campbell."

At the wedding supper in the elegant ballroom of a hotel in New Orleans—the home base of

Dreamweavers, Inc. and the Sinclair family—Josh sat in bemused silence watching Charlie and Kate Sinclair preside over their colorful brood.

Josh smiled as his glance went from Kate to each of her daughters in turn. There might have been precious little feminine influence in his early life, he thought, but things had definitely changed. And he couldn't have been happier. Kate was the mother of everyone's dreams, and Heather's sisters were as beautiful, vibrant, and full of beans as Josh had known they would be.

His gaze locked in on his wife, ethereally lovely in a drift of white chiffon, the soft fabric falling from her shoulders in gently draped folds over her breasts, nipped in at her slender waist by a wide satin band studded with tiny pearls. Her hair was caught up in a circlet of heather blossoms from her bridal bouquet. Maharg had arranged for her namesake flowers to be flown over from Scotland.

"Are you thinking that you signed on with a pretty boisterous crew?" Heather asked. Josh was quiet, and she wondered if he felt overwhelmed by so many new relatives.

"I'm thinking I signed on with a pretty terrific crew," he answered, quickly adding, "Watch it, honey . . ."

Heather laughed as she realized that the flowing sleeves of her gown, attractive as they might be, were a bit difficult to manage at a dinner table. Reaching for the salt, she'd knocked over the heavy crystal shaker. As she picked it up, she instinctively raised it to toss some of its contents over her shoulder, but stopped midsprinkle. "I've given up that sort of thing," she told Josh proudly as she put the shaker back on the table.

He grinned, leaned over to brush his lips over hers, then picked up the salt shaker and threw a few grains over his own shoulder. "What the hell," he said with a chuckle. "You can't be too careful."

Heather laughed delightedly and fell in love all over again.

Much as he enjoyed the reception, complete with Cajun and Scottish fiddle music, Josh was overjoyed when the moment arrived to whisk Heather away to begin their honeymoon.

With a few tips from Lisa's husband, Josh had managed to do to Heather what Pete had done to Lisa for their going-away trip—he'd kept the plans a secret from the bride. He was confident she would love the reception Maharg was going to throw in Edinburgh, and she was going to be thrilled with the castle hideaway he'd scouted out for a stay on the misty, legend-rich Isle of Skye, but the element of surprise was important.

Meanwhile, for their first night as husband and wife, Josh had reserved the bridal suite at an old French Quarter hotel, luxurious and supposedly haunted. He'd had their luggage moved to their rooms earlier in the day.

"What a wonderful place," Heather said, admiring the silk wall coverings, the high ceilings, the rich carpeting of the hallway.

Josh unlocked the gilt-trimmed ivory door and pushed it open. "Well, Muffin, are you ready to be carried over the threshold into your new life?"

She grinned at him, her whole being alive with excitement. "You still won't tell me where we're going?"

He wagged his head slowly from side to side. "You'll find out soon enough, Mrs. Campbell."

"So another part of Annie's dream comes true, does it? The fair-haired giant of a man carries me off to unknown places without so much as a by-your-leave? And makes a *Campbell* of me, no less?"

Josh nodded. "But you've left out a part."

"What part?" Heather asked, cocking her head to one side in genuine curiosity.

Suddenly Josh bent, curved his arm around Heather's legs, and unceremoniously flung her over his shoulder. "This part," he said as he strode into the suite, pushed the door shut, and carried Heather into the bedroom to toss her onto the soft mattress of the four-poster bed, stretching out over her.

Laughing helplessly, Heather twined her arms around her husband's neck, then grew quiet, smiling up at him, her eyes filled with love. "Does this mean you're always going to make my dreams come true?" she asked softly.

Josh held her with one arm while reaching up to take the combs and pins and flowers from her hair. "Just the good ones," he answered, spreading her silken curls out over the pillow to frame her face in a halo of fire. Then, lowering his mouth to hers, he added, "Which is only fair, since you're just about to do the same for me."

THE EDITOR'S CORNER

As is the case with many of you, LOVESWEPT books have been a part of my life for a very long time—since before we ever published book #1, in fact. Having worked with Carolyn Nichols for over seven years, there's no way I could not have been caught up in her enthusiasm for and devotion to the LOVESWEPT project. I hope I can convey my excitement over the wonderful books we publish as entertainingly as Carolyn has over the years in the Editor's Corner.

Since next month is April, we're going to shower you with "keepers." Our six books for the month are sure to coax the sun from behind the clouds and brighten your rainy days.

Continuing her *Once Upon a Time* series, Kay Hooper brings you **WHAT DREAMS MAY COME**, LOVESWEPT #390. Can you imagine what Kelly Russell goes through when, a week before her wedding, her fiancé, John Mitchell, has a tragic accident which leaves him in a coma? Ten years later Kelly is finally putting the past behind her when Mitch arrives on her doorstep, determined to rekindle the love that fate had stolen from them. Kay involves the reader from page one in this poignant, modern-day Rip Van Winkle story. Your emotions will run the gamut as you root for brave survivor Kelly and enigmatic Mitch to bridge the chasm of time and build a new life together.

Sandra Chastain has the remarkable ability to create vivid characters with winning personalities. Her people always lead interesting, purposeful lives—and the hero and heroine in **ADAM'S OUTLAW**, LOVESWEPT #391, are no exceptions. Toni Gresham leads a group of concerned citizens called Peachtree Vigilantes, who are out to corral muggers who prey on the elderly. Instead she swoops down from a tree with a Tarzan yell and lands atop police captain Adam Ware! Adam, who is conducting his own sting operation, is stunned to discover he's being held captive by an angel with golden curls. You'll laugh as the darling renegade tries to teach the lone-wolf lawman a thing or two about helping people—and in return learns a thing or two about love.

I suggest saving Janet Evanovich's **SMITTEN**, LOVESWEPT #392, for one of those rainy days this month. There's no way that after reading this gem of a romance you won't be smiling and floating on air! Single mom Lizabeth Kane wasn't exactly construction worker material, but she

(continued)

figured she could learn. The hours were good—she'd be home by the time her kids were out of school—and the location—the end of her block—was convenient. Matt Hallahan takes one look at her résumé—handwritten on spiral notebook paper—then at the lady herself, and he's instantly smitten. When the virile hunk agrees to hire her, Lizabeth's heart—and her libido—send up a cheer! Lizabeth never knew that painting a wall could be a sensual experience or that the smell of sawdust could be so enticing, but whenever Matt was near, he made her senses sizzle. Janet adds some zany secondary characters to this tender story who are guaranteed to make you laugh. For an uplifting experience, don't miss **SMITTEN!**

April showers occasionally leave behind rainbows. Tami Hoag brings you one rainbow this month and two more over the next several months in the form of her three-book series, *The Rainbow Chasers*. The Fearsome Foursome was what they called themselves, four college friends who bonded together and shared dreams of pursuing their hearts' desires in a sleepy coastal town in northern California. In **HEART OF GOLD**, LOVESWEPT #393, Tami picks up on the lives of the friends as one by one they realize their dreams and find the ends of their personal rainbows. Faith Kincaid is just about to open her inn and begin to forget her former life in Washington, D.C., when elegantly handsome Shane Callan—Dirty Harry in disguise—arrives on assignment to protect her—a government witness in a bribery trial. Faith has never known the intoxicating feeling of having a man want her until Shane pulls her to him on a darkened staircase and makes her yearn for the taste of his lips. Shane, lonely and haunted by demons, realizes Faith is his shot at sanctuary, his anchor in the storm. **HEART OF GOLD** is a richly textured story that you won't be able to put down. But Tami's next in the series won't be far behind! Look for **KEEPING COMPANY** in June and **REILLY'S RETURN** in August. You can spend the entire summer chasing rainbows!

Courtney Henke is one of the brightest new stars on the LOVESWEPT horizon. And for those of you who wrote after reading her first book, **CHAMELEON**, asking for Adam's story, Courtney has granted your wish—and delivered one sensational story in **JINX**, LOVESWEPT #394. How much

(continued)

more romantic can you get than a hero who falls in love with the heroine even before he meets her? It's Diana Machlen's ethereal image in an advertisement for the perfume her family developed that haunts Adam's dreams. But the lady in the flesh is just as tempting, when Adam—on a mission to retrieve from her the only written copy of the perfume formula—encounters the lovely Diana at her cabin in the Missouri Ozarks. Diana greets Adam less than enthusiastically. You see, strange things happen when she gets close to a man—and there's no way she can stay away from Adam! The chain of events is just too funny for words as Adam vows to prove her wrong about her jinx. Don't miss this delightful romp!

Deborah Smith's name has been popping up in more and more of your letters as one of the favorite LOVESWEPT authors. It's no wonder! Deborah has an imagination and creative ability that knows no bounds. In **LEGENDS,** LOVE-SWEPT #395, Deborah wisks you from a penthouse in Manhattan to a tiny village in Scotland. At a lavish party billionaire Douglas Kincaid can't help but follow the mysterious woman in emerald silk onto his terrace. Elgiva MacRoth wants the brutally handsome dealmaker—but only to kidnap him! She holds him captive in order to preserve her heritage and convince him to give up his land holdings in Scotland. But soon it's not clear who is the prisoner and who is the jailer as Douglas melts her resistance and revels in her sensuality. These two characters are so alive, they almost walk right off the pages. Deborah will have you believing in legends before you finish this mesmerizing story.

Look for our sparkling violet covers next month, and enjoy a month of great reading with LOVESWEPT!

Sincerely,

Susann Brailey

Susann Brailey
Editor
LOVESWEPT
Bantam Books
666 Fifth Avenue
New York, NY 10103

FAN OF THE MONTH

Kay Bendall

What a thrill and an honor to be selected a LOVE-SWEPT Fan of the Month! Reading is one of the joys of my life. Through books I enter worlds of enchantment, wonder, adventure, suspense, beauty, fantasy, humor, and, above all else, a place where love conquers all.

My favorite books are LOVESWEPTs. Each and every month I am impressed and delighted with the variety and excellence of the selections. I laugh, cry, am inspired, touched, and enjoy them all.

Kay Hooper, Joan Elliott Pickart, Iris Johansen, Deborah Smith, Barbara Boswell, and Peggy Webb are some of my favorite LOVESWEPT authors. The blend of familiar and new authors ensure that LOVESWEPTs will remain innovative and number one among the romance books.

The day the mailman brings my LOVESWEPTs is my favorite day of the month!

OFFICIAL RULES TO
LOVESWEPT'S
DREAM MAKER GIVEAWAY
(See entry card in center of this book)

1. NO PURCHASE NECESSARY. To enter both the sweepstakes and accept the risk-free trial offer, follow the directions published on the insert card in this book. Return your entry on the reply card provided. If you do not wish to take advantage of the risk-free trial offer, but wish to enter the sweepstakes, return the entry card only with the "FREE ENTRY" sticker attached, or send your name and address on a 3x5 card to : Loveswept Sweepstakes, Bantam Books, PO Box 985, Hicksville, NY 11802-9827.

2. To be eligible for the prizes offered, your entry must be received by September 17, 1990. We are not responsible for late, lost or misdirected mail. Winners will be selected on or about October 16, 1990 in a random drawing under the supervision of Marden Kane, Inc., an independent judging organization, and except for those prizes which will be awarded to the first 50 entrants, prizes will be awarded after that date. By entering this sweepstakes, each entrant accepts and agrees to be bound by these rules and the decision of the judges which shall be final and binding. This sweepstakes will be presented in conjunction with various book offers sponsored by Bantam Books under the following titles: Agatha Christie "Mystery Showcase", Louis L'Amour "Great American Getaway", Loveswept "Dreams Can Come True" and Loveswept "Dream Makers". Although the prize options and graphics of this Bantam Books sweepstakes will vary in each of these book offers, the value of each prize level will be approximately the same and prize winners will have the options of selecting any prize offered within the prize level won.

3. Prizes in the Loveswept "Dream Maker" sweepstakes: Grand Prize (1) 14 Day trip to either Hawaii, Europe or the Caribbean. Trip includes round trip air transportation from any major airport in the US and hotel accomodations (approximate retail value $6,000); Bonus Prize (1) $1,000 cash in addition to the trip; Second Prize (1) 27" Color TV (approximate retail value $900).

4. This sweepstakes is open to residents of the US, and Canada (excluding the province of Quebec), who are 18 years of age or older. Employees of Bantam Books, Bantam Doubleday Dell Publishing Group Inc., their affiliates and subsidiaries, Marden Kane Inc. and all other agencies and persons connected with conducting this sweepstakes and their immediate family members are not eligible to enter this sweepstakes. This offer is subject to all applicable laws and regulations and is void in the province of Quebec and wherever prohibited or restricted by law. In order to win a prize, residents of Canada will be required to correctly answer a time-limited arithmetical skill-testing question.

5. Winners will be notified by mail and will be required to execute an affidavit of eligibility and release which must be returned within 14 days of notification or an alternate winner will be selected. Prizes are not transferable. Trip prize must be taken within one year of notification and is subject to airline departure schedules and ticket and accommodation availability. Winner must have a valid passport. No substitution will be made for any prize except as offered. If a prize should be unavailable at sweepstakes end, sponsor reserves the right to substitute a prize of equal or greater value. Winners agree that the sponsor, its affiliates, and their agencies and employees shall not be liable for injury, loss or damage of any kind resulting from an entrant's participation in this offer or from the acceptance or use of the prizes awarded. Odds of winning are dependant upon the number of entries received. Taxes, if any, are the sole responsibility of the winners. Winner's entry and acceptance of any prize offered constitutes permission to use the winner's name, photograph or other likeness for purposes of advertising and promotion on behalf of Bantam Books and Bantam Doubleday Dell Publishing Group Inc. without additional compensation to the winner.

6. For a list of winners (available after 10/16/90), send a self addressed stamped envelope to Bantam Books Winners List, PO Box 704, Sayreville, NJ 08871.

7. The free gifts are available only to entrants who also agree to sample the Loveswept subscription program on the terms described. The sweepstakes prizes offered by affixing the "Free Entry" sticker to the Entry Form are available to all entrants, whether or not an entrant chooses to affix the "Free Books" sticker to the Entry Form.

60 Minutes to a Better, More Beautiful You!

Now it's easier than ever to awaken your sensuality, stay slim forever—even make yourself irresistible. With Bantam's bestselling subliminal audio tapes, you're only 60 minutes away from a better, more beautiful you!

__ 45004-2	**Slim Forever**	$8.95
__ 45112-X	**Awaken Your Sensuality**	$7.95
__ 45081-6	**You're Irresistible**	$7.95
__ 45035-2	**Stop Smoking Forever**	$8.95
__ 45130-8	**Develop Your Intuition**	$7.95
__ 45022-0	**Positively Change Your Life**	$8.95
__ 45154-5	**Get What You Want**	$7.95
__ 45041-7	**Stress Free Forever**	$7.95
__ 45106-5	**Get a Good Night's Sleep**	$7.95
__ 45094-8	**Improve Your Concentration**	$7.95
__ 45172-3	**Develop A Perfect Memory**	$8.95

Bantam Books, Dept. LT, 414 East Golf Road, Des Plaines, IL 60016

Please send me the items I have checked above. I am enclosing $_____
(please add $2.00 to cover postage and handling). Send check or money
order, no cash or C.O.D.s please. (Tape offer good in USA only.)

Mr/Ms _____

Address _____

City/State _____ Zip_____

LT-12/89

Please allow four to six weeks for delivery.
Prices and availability subject to change without notice.